Donald a. Wilson

THE
WALTON BOYS

and

Rapids Ahead

By
HAL BURTON

Illustrated by
ROBERT DOREMUS

★

WHITMAN PUBLISHING COMPANY
RACINE, WISCONSIN

CONTENTS

ILLUSTRATIONS

"Well, What Goes on Here?"

THE WALTON BOYS
and
Rapids Ahead

CHAPTER ONE

VACATION PLANS

"Where's everybody?" Bert Walton called as he let the screen door bang behind him. It was exceptionally quiet for a spring evening in the Walton household. And the exhilarated Bert, fresh from a victorious softball game, wondered at it. The only sound he could hear was a faint rustling of paper that seemed to come from the living-room. He ran one finger through his bristling red hair, wrinkled his brow perplexedly, and called again, "Hey!" Still no sound but the rustling of paper. It was almost scary and he felt compelled to walk softly.

"Well, I'll be jiggered!" he exclaimed as he poked his head through the living-room archway. The floor was covered with stacks of maps and shiny booklets. In the center of all this were his two brothers. Ed, the sixteen-year-old, was stretched out full-length raptly contemplating a colored picture of a rushing river. Howard, the thirteen-year-old, and one year Bert's junior, was sitting cross-legged while he used

11

one finger to trace a route along a map he held. Both of them glanced up briefly as Bert hesitated in the doorway.

"Well, what goes on here?" demanded Bert. "Doesn't anybody want to ask me how the game came out? We won, if you're interested."

Ed glanced up again at Bert. "Never mind," he said, "we're busy making some plans."

"Do they include me?" Bert asked eagerly.

"You bet they do." His older brother laughed, handing him a bundle of booklets. "Look these over and help us decide where to spend our vacation this summer."

"Boy!" shouted Bert. "I can think of nothing I'd like better!" He riffled through the booklets. "But all of these are from Maine! Just what kind of vacation are you thinking about?"

"A canoeing trip, of course," Ed answered. "What could be finer? A month up in the northern forests, rapids to shoot, fish to catch—doesn't it sound good?"

Bert glanced inside one folder before replying slowly. "Of course it does, I just hadn't thought much about it."

"Boy, look at this!" Howard broke in, holding up a picture. It was a photograph of three boys in a canoe dropping down through a swirling rapids, a rapids so steep that it seemed a waterfall.

"Yeah," Bert agreed finally. "Looks mighty good.

But we haven't got a canoe. What are we going to do, swim down the river or make ourselves a raft?"

"What you mean, bud," explained Ed, "is that we didn't have a canoe when you left the house after supper tonight. If you hadn't been in such a hurry, I could have told you. I went down to Wilson's Hardware this morning and ordered an eighteen-foot metal canoe. All these years that we've been paddling around the river here, we've been using someone else's canoe. Well, obviously, we couldn't go to Maine in a borrowed canoe, so pretty soon we'll have our own."

"Swell!" said Bert, but he couldn't keep an expression of doubt from his face. "Only thing is, do we know that these metal canoes are any good?"

"Why, of course they are," Ed assured him, pushing himself up on his elbows as he talked. He picked his way across the room through the welter of paper, holding a booklet in his hand. "Here's the proof."

Bert looked at the booklet. "Well, looks all right."

"Not only looks all right, but is all right," observed Ed. "I checked up on it pretty carefully. It's all well riveted, and there are two sealed air chambers in either end. Even if you tip the canoe over or fill it with water, you can't possibly sink it."

"And when can we start practicing with it?" asked Bert, finally convinced.

"Up in Maine, when we begin our trip," his older

brother answered. "I'm having it shipped there. School is finished this Friday, and on Saturday morning we'll get on the train for Coboscus Lake. From there, that is if you agree, we'll start back into the woods and down the Seboomook River. It'll take us nearly a month if we explore along the way."

"Sounds better and better," burst out Bert. "And, of course, I needn't ask if we can afford it." He chuckled.

"Well, with a gold mine out in Utah piling up money for us, I guess we can spend a little on this trip," Ed replied. "I wanted to get your okay on this vacation because, since you found the mine, you might say that you have the first claim on the money."

"Well, maybe I found it," Bert said thoughtfully, "but you fellows found me. Remember, Tom Wallace, the old prospector, had locked me up in the mine. If you hadn't come along to rescue me, I might be there yet." He shivered a little and seemed to feel himself back in the icy stillness of the Utah mountains. He looked gratefully up at Ed, and then across at Howard, on whose face was a wide grin.

"I've often thought," teased Howard, "that I could have made you jump six feet by standing outside the living-room window with a mackinaw and a soft hat on. You'd surely have thought I was Wallace."

"Oh, no," Bert shot back. "I'd have figured you were my brother Howard, playing another practical joke. Tom Wallace went out of our lives when I accidentally knocked loose that snow avalanche. He was directly underneath it, and I know he couldn't have escaped."

"Well, then suppose I'd put on a cap and a tweed jacket and stood outside there," persisted Howard, pointing toward the shimmering darkness outside the big picture window. "You'd have thought I was Alan Wallace."

"That could be," said Bert, agreeing for once. "Because Alan got away, and the last we heard of him he was on his way to New England by plane. That was three months ago, you know, but we haven't heard of him, and I'll bet we won't. He's too scared to try to pull any more tricks on us."

"Well, maybe," broke in Ed.

Outside the window, as Bert settled down to study the route of the canoe trip more thoroughly, the long New England twilight began to give way to full darkness. Bert had been playing hard, and he was almost dozing when he thought he heard a faint, almost imperceptible footstep on the porch.

"Did you hear that?" he asked his brothers in a stage whisper. Two startled faces swung round and looked toward the picture window. Bert listened intently. He couldn't be sure whether it was the thudding of his own heart, or whether he actually heard another footstep.

"Ah, it's nothing," said Howard loudly, and swung back to the maps he was reading. Ed, by this time seated in a chair, shrugged his shoulders. His lips formed the words, *Just imagination,* and Bert fell into his half-doze again. He was awakened from it, by the crackle of paper as Howard briskly began to fold maps and stack booklets.

"Me for bed," he announced as he walked out the door. His footsteps could be heard on the staircase, followed by the slam of the door as he swung into his own room.

"Don't let your imagination run away with you, kid," Ed advised Bert. "The Wallaces are gone from our lives. I thought I heard something, too, but I know perfectly well that the only people who'll be coming up onto our porch at this hour will be Mother and Dad, back from the bridge game."

"Yeah, I guess I'll forget about it," Bert said slowly. "But, just the same—" he ran his hand through his bristling hair, "I would have sworn that I heard someone out there."

"Well, now that Howie's gone, let's settle down to do some planning," Ed suggested. "I've got the rations pretty well figured out, and here's the list. See what you think." He held out a penciled envelope, on which he had been scribbling. Bert took it from his hand, and let out a low whistle. "Sounds like enough food to feed an army."

"Yeah, if we were going out only a week, it would be, too," his brother agreed. "But we're going for a month, and we'll be mighty hungry after a day's canoeing."

Bert shuddered. "What bothers me is not the last part of the trip, but the first part. Just think of toting all this stuff over the portages!"

"It will be tough the first few days," agreed his brother, "but after that, you'll get used to it. Remember that pack down in the basement with the peculiar strap attached to it?" Bert nodded assent. "Well, that strap's a tumpline. I used one two summers ago, the time I went to the lakes in northern New Hampshire when you and Howard were down on the coast near Gloucester. You put that tumpline around your forehead, lean against it, and it takes half the load off your shoulders."

"And breaks your neck in the process?" Bert chuckled.

"Well, I must admit that it feels that way at the beginning," agreed his older brother with a smile, "but once your neck muscles are toughened, it's not bad at all."

"At least I'll come back in good shape for football." Bert flexed his muscles. "So there'll be some good out of this trip."

"Right you are." Ed chuckled. "But if you don't get to bed tonight, you'll be in bad shape for the canoe trip." He bent down and scooped up the remaining folders on the floor; then stacked them neatly with the collection Howard has assembled on the table beside Bert.

"Aw, let me take just a few minutes longer to read some of these other booklets," pleaded Bert.

Ed left, and Bert was halfway down the Seboomook River in his imagination, when he heard a faint creaking on the porch again. His back was to the window, and he was almost afraid to turn around. He forced himself to do so, however. All he could see was the glitter of light reflected from the lamp beside him. It was hard to do, but he reached up and flicked the switch on the lamp. Then, turning his chair, he half-faced the window.

For a moment Bert's eyes could not accustom themselves to the darkness outside. Then he could see the spiky outline of the two cedar trees that grew just beyond the porch railing. He sighed with relief. There was nothing between them—nothing, until a threatening figure slowly rose just outside the window. He could see two hands, flattened against the reverse side of the pane, and an indistinct face, a slouch hat, and some sort of jacket.

"Tom Wallace!" he breathed in terror. And then he laughed. "Howie!" he called. "Howie!" he re-

peated in a louder voice. "You idiot! You can't fool me!"

Bert sprinted for the door, skidded across a throw rug on the waxed floor of the hallway, and plunged out through the screen door. Howie, or whoever it was, had started to run across the lawn, weaving in and out of the shadows, and then veering suddenly toward the back yard. Bert plunged after him. He had untied his shoelaces and they flapped behind him as he quickened his pace.

"Howie!" he shouted. "Quit kidding! Come back here!" Over his head, a window was flung up, and he could hear someone calling to him, but he was too engrossed in the chase to listen. He had almost caught up to the fleeing figure when he tripped and fell headlong. The grass was cool and resilient, and the fall did him no harm. As he picked himself up, he could see the figure vaulting over the picket fence that separated the back yard from a narrow alley-way. He made a leap for the high fence, and just cleared its wooden spikes. As his feet touched the gravel, he looked swiftly around. The mysterious fugitive was nowhere in sight. To his left, the alley came to a dead end at the half-opened door of Johnson's old barn. When he was smaller, Bert had loved to explore its musty interior, still redolent of horses and hay. Now, it occurred to him that Howard had shared this fondness for the barn, abandoned as it was, with rotting floors and treacherous stairs. He strode swiftly to the half-opened door and ducked inside.

"Come on, Howie," he said cajolingly. "I'm not mad. Howie!" In the silence that followed his words, he could hear someone breathing heavily, not many feet away from him. A terrible thought occurred to him. *If this really was Howard, why doesn't he answer?* A lump crowded up in his throat, and then he took a step forward into the blackness, his hands outstretched. One hand brushed a woolly surface, and then a face. As he recoiled, with a gasp, someone brushed by him, was silhouetted for a moment in the dim light of the doorway, and then disappeared into the alleyway with crunching steps. All the mirth went out of Bert as he stood stock still for a moment.

The face he had touched was bearded, a stubbly, scraggy beard, such as Tom Wallace wore. Momentarily, he felt a paralyzing fear; then he dove for the door and sprinted down the alley to its junction with the street. His quarry had gone. There was nothing to be seen but a dimly lighted thoroughfare without a soul on it. Digging the toes of his shoes into the gravel, he walked thoughtfully back to the picket fence. Beyond it, he could hear the voices of both his brothers; and, through it, he saw the gleam of a flashlight.

"He must have gone this way," Ed was saying.

"Over the fence, I guess. And, look here, he tore a chunk from his mackinaw."

Bert stepped back, took a running leap into space, and landed lightly beside his brothers.

"I thought it was you, Howie," he said to his astonished younger brother. "But it wasn't. It was Tom Wallace. I accidentally touched his face when he was hiding in the barn. And this is part of his mackinaw. I'd remember that color combination for a thousand years. He's around somewhere, and he means trouble for us. We'd better find Dad and tell him."

CHAPTER TWO

THE TWO STRANGERS

Downstairs Bert could hear the familiar tinkling of glasses and the rattling of breakfast dishes. He rose on his elbow and looked around him, as if to reassure himself that he was indeed in his own room. The night had never seemed so long, nor his dreams so confusing. He sighed, sank back on his pillow, and launched himself on the rippling waters of another, pleasanter dream.

This trip into dreamland started on a Maine river. Then, somehow, he was paddling beneath a roaring waterfall. Oddly enough, the water fell one drop at a time. He bowed his head and then put his hands over his face to keep out the water, but now it was trickling down his neck. He woke with a start. Howard, scrubbed, brushed, and shining, was standing beside his bed, squeezing a sponge so that it dripped down on him. Spluttering, Bert jumped out onto the floor, landing with a thump.

Howard, by this time, had fled to the safety of the door. "Better hurry," he said. "Almost time for school, and Dad wants to talk to us."

Bert started to dress hastily, noticing that the

clock said eight. He threw on his clothes, laced his shoes, dashed into the bathroom and dabbed at his face. He came down the steps, and hurried into the dining-room.

Mr. Walton put down his coffee cup. "I'll talk while you eat, Bert. The other boys are almost finished."

"Yes, sir," Bert mumbled shamefacedly. "I guess I didn't hear the others get up."

Mr. Walton, a broad-shouldered man with a ruddy complexion, leaned forward in his chair to emphasize what he had to say. "I heard what happened last night, Bert," he said in a deep, impressive voice. "Don't let it worry you. This is a small town, and strangers are easy to detect. I have already phoned Constable Brown; he's checked the hotel, and is looking around in the hobo jungle down by the railroad yards. He'll keep an eye on you when you get on the train; and, of course, I will go down to see you off. Just go along to school as if nothing had happened."

"All right, sir," said Bert. "I will. I still am finding it hard to realize that Wallace is alive; but if he is, I'm not afraid of him." He pushed back his chair, said good-by to his father, and left for school. Ed and Howard had already started out, and Bert strolled along, whistling tunelessly. He slipped in behind his desk just a second before the final morning bell rang insistently.

In the interval between English and math, he strolled down the hallway and looked out the door. Across the street, in front of the stationery store, a figure was lounging. Bert was unable to decide whether the man at whom he looked was staring back at him, or simply looking idly at the building. A sudden inspiration occurred to him. He'd bait a trap.

He stepped out onto the fire escape, and into the weak sunlight. The lounging figure seemed to jump, and then ducked back into the doorway. The sound of the bell, signaling the next class, sent Bert puzzling on his way. Could he have seen Wallace again? And, more important, had Wallace seen him?

After lunch in the cafeteria, as Bert trudged up to his last classes, he could hear the distant roll of thunder, and then the drumming sound of rain.

Heck, Bert thought to himself, *and I didn't bring a raincoat with me!* At the next recess, he ran hastily down a floor and sought out Ed.

"Sure, I brought my raincoat," said his older brother. "Figured this might happen. We'll wrap up in the coat together and get home somehow."

Bert said a hasty thank you and sprinted upstairs again. It seemed as if the afternoon would never end, but suddenly the dismissal bell echoed through the halls.

"Okay, let's go," Bert's older brother said to him as he met him a few minutes later. "On the way home, we've got to make one stop. We'll go over to the railroad station and get our tickets."

Clumsily wrapped in the folds of the same raincoat, the two boys made their way to the corner, where rain had collected in a huge puddle. "We'd better cross a little way up the block," Ed said, and the two boys moved fifty feet up the curbing. It was raining harder now, and most of the passing cars had turned on their lights. Bert stared up the street, on the alert for traffic, but Ed kept his eyes straight ahead. A steady string of cars splashed by, and then there was a momentary lull.

"Okay now," Ed noted. Bert lagged a bit behind as they stepped off the curb, and habit again prompted him to look up the street. Out of the murk, its lights not burning, slid a small, sleek auto, whose windshield was covered with raindrops. It seemed to Bert, somehow, that this car was running far closer to the curb than the others had been. Involuntarily, he cried, "Look out!" and yanked Ed backward over the curb. Both boys fell in a huddle on the damp ground.

The car had come within an inch of hurtling the curb. It would have hit them head-on if they had not stepped back.

"They—they meant to hit us!" Bert gasped as he

got to his feet again.

His older brother, noticeably pale, nodded his head. "You may be right. That could be Wallace, or it could be Alan. Whoever it was, either wanted to run us down or was terribly careless." He took a deep breath, and put his arm around Bert's shoulder. "They can't scare us, and they haven't hurt us. Let's keep on to the station, boy."

The storm was beginning to diminish in fury, and a watery sun was peeking through a rift in the clouds. Soon the torrent of rain dwindled to a drizzle, and, by the time Bert and his brother had reached the red brick railway station, the sun was glittering from the steel rails. The waiting-room, with its fumed oak benches and dusty smell, was bare of passengers. The station agent, old Mr. Howland, dozed behind his grille. Bert shuffled his feet and coughed tentatively.

"Oh-uh-hello, boys," the station agent said, blinking his eyes. "I was expectin' you in here to buy your tickets, but I didn't figger you'd be here so soon."

"How'd you know we were going anywhere?" Bert demanded. He wheeled on his brother. "Ed, have you been down here before, checking up on tickets?"

"Why—why, no!" his older brother stammered, and Bert could see that he also was surprised. "I didn't think it was necessary."

"*Ed, Have You Been Down Here Before?*"

"Well, 'twasn't one of you boys who told me," grunted the gray-haired station agent. "A young fella in a tweed coat came in the middle of the day, and asked if you Waltons were goin' on a trip. And then, a little later, Constable Brown came by—" He stopped, struck with an idea. "Say," he asked, "what sort of funny business is goin' on here? Strangers askin' fer you, and then Constable Brown askin' fer strangers. I don't get it."

"What kind of stranger did he want to know about?" asked Bert.

"Oh, an old feller, wearin' a mackinaw with a tear in it," the station agent answered. "Said he'd been botherin' some folks around town, but didn't tell me who."

"See?" said Bert triumphantly, turning to face his brother, "I told you so."

"Right you are," Ed agreed, "but let's not keep Mr. Howland waiting. Mr. Howland, we want three coach tickets to Seboomook, Maine." It took the old man a long time, but finally he shoved the tickets through the window, accepted some money in return, and immediately fell into his doze again.

Bert nudged his brother. "That description sounds like Alan," he said. "Bet a dollar both of them are hanging around here somewhere."

"Maybe," Ed agreed, "but in that case, if they don't know where we're going, it might be a lot better for us to go ahead with our vacation. They'll never find us up in the north woods. There's too much country up there."

It was just a step down the street to the constable's office. Through the plate-glass window, Bert could see Constable Brown, his half-bald head bent over some papers. He tapped timidly at the door, and a booming "Come in" answered his signal. Brown, an immensely fat man with a broad, beaming face, nodded kindly to them.

"I know what you're asking about, and you don't need to worry. I went across the tracks, into the hobo jungle, because I figured your friend Wallace might hide out there. I had a little trouble getting the information I needed, but finally one young fellow spoke up. He said that a man answering Wallace's description had gotten on a southbound freight this morning. That would take him back to Boston and out of the way."

"I suppose so," Bert agreed, "but the trouble is, he has a son, and his son was down at the railroad station this morning, asking about us."

Constable Brown let out a low whistle, and a cloud spread across his face. "Well," he finally said, "that does complicate matters a little. But just so long as the boy can't find out where you're going, I don't see that you have any reason to worry. Just go home and forget about it now. I'll keep an eye on your house tonight, and I'll be around the station in the morning to make sure nobody's spying on you."

"Thanks," said Bert, and meant it. He backed toward the door, almost tripping over Ed, and then walked out again on the street. In the sunlight, with familiar faces everywhere he looked, the whole thought of the Wallaces seemed, somehow, like a nightmare.

Raindrops shimmered on the lawn of the Walton home as Bert and Ed strolled up the sidewalk. Ed sprinted up the steps onto the porch, but Bert lagged behind.

"I think I'll just take a look around and see if that visitor of ours last night left any other clues," he called to his older brother.

Ed shook his head in mock despair. "Always the detective, aren't you?"

Bert waved his hand in farewell and started around the house. The rain had washed any footprints out of the grass or the few bare spots beside the trees. He turned to go back in the front door, and then his wandering eye lit on something. A muddy spot, directly under the dining-room window, had been disturbed. Very carefully, he walked over to it.

There, in the mud, were two sets of footprints, one deeper than the other. Sometime toward the end of the storm, somebody had crouched beneath the

window, spying on the people inside! Being careful
not to disturb the impressions in the mud, he set
one of his feet alongside the tracks. The length of
the shoes was almost identical.

"Alan," he half-whispered to himself. And then
all his curiosity disappeared. He simply wanted to
be inside the house, and he made it on the run.

CHAPTER THREE

AN UNEXPECTED RIDE

Sometime late that night, Bert woke from a sound sleep and sat bolt upright. Across the room he could hear Howard's soft, measured breathing, and he felt a twinge of envy at his brother's calm ability to drowse off. In the dim moonlight, slanting through the open window, he could see outlined the packs and duffle bags for tomorrow's trip. Somewhere, far off, a dog barked, and then there was the faint, sad whistle of a train, and the growing beam of its headlight as it rounded the curve north of town and pounded down to the station. That same headlight, Bert thought to himself, was right now sweeping across the alder bushes down by the river where the hoboes made camp. Once or twice, coming home from a school play or the movies by a roundabout way, he had seen the flicker of their campfires and had heard the sound of their voices.

Tonight, perhaps, mingling with these men, was Alan Wallace, his enemy. The thought made him restless, and he squirmed uneasily. He thought back to the time, months before, in Utah, when his curiosity had nearly killed him. But more powerful in his mind was the feeling that he had to know if Alan was near. He had to find out, and he would find out!

Very quietly he swung his feet out of bed and reached down for his shoes and socks. He slipped his shirt and trousers on over his pajamas, picked up his shoes, and tiptoed silently out through the door. The whole house was perfectly still. He trod carefully, going down the stairway, remembering that the third and sixth treads were squeaky. The screen door opened noiselessly to his touch; his father had oiled it the day before. On the porch dew had collected; it felt cool to his bare feet, but he did not dare to sit down and put on his socks and shoes until he felt the gritty coldness of the sidewalk beneath his soles.

Still walking carefully, Bert made his way down the street. The clock on the Methodist church said 11:30 p.m., and nearly everyone in town was in bed. On Main Street, a light still burned in a law office, but the street lamps had been dimmed. He was walking rapidly now, and his footsteps echoed hollowly on the deserted street. Only a short distance around the corner, a faint light burned in the railroad station, and a row of boxcars stood motionless on a siding. Bert made his way carefully through the maze of tracks, looked in both directions to make sure no engine was attached to the boxcars, and then squeezed through underneath the air hose and the coupling between two cars. As he stood upright, on the far side, he could see the campfires down by the river; and, in the moonlight, a narrow path leading down through the marsh. He found himself shivering, but he resolutely walked down the path.

In a clearing, perhaps a hundred feet beyond the tracks, but shielded from the station by an alder thicket, a big campfire was blazing. A husky young man in a sweater was crouched beside it, warming his hands. He looked up as Bert approached, but he did not seem surprised to have a visitor.

He stood up, as if welcoming a guest, and said in a deep voice, "Well, sonny, what's your trouble? Don't tell me you've run away from home?"

Bert had been prepared to run, to dislike this stranger, or to do anything except what he did. He sat down on a projecting log and began to explain the purpose of his visit.

"I'm Red Smith," said the young hobo, sticking out his hand for Bert to shake. "I've been down East here, looking for work, but now I'm going back home to the Midwest again to settle down. Now, tell me the rest of your story." As Bert continued, Smith raised his eyebrows and whistled soundlessly at one point, as if something had just occurred to him.

"Sounds like a detective story," he said when Bert had finished, "and maybe there's something I can tell you. But first, have a little tea. I just brewed it myself." Bert accepted the cup gratefully and gulped down a mouthful of tea while waiting for Red Smith to continue.

"The young fellow you talk about," explained Smith, "or someone very much like him, was down here not less than an hour ago asking for his dad. I told him the last I saw of the old man, he was getting ready to catch a freight bound for Boston. He mumbled something about not believing me, so I told him if he wanted to, he could go look through those empty cars up on the side track there. He went walking up that way, and that was the end of it. Maybe he's still around up there. I wouldn't know." He yawned elaborately, stretched his arms, and leaned back against a tree trunk.

"Well, you'd better run along home now, sonny," he said between yawns. "Your folks will be missing you, and me—I need some sleep." He closed his eyes and nodded drowsily.

Bert murmured, "Gee, thanks, Red," and started reluctantly up the path to the railroad tracks.

The moonlight played strange tricks on Bert's eyesight that night. As he came up to the siding, and looked down the line of boxcars, most of them with doors wide open, he felt sure that he saw a shadowy figure dodge into one car far down the track.

Now don't be foolish, he said to himself. *Remember what happened before—* But the next thing he knew, he was walking swiftly down the line of cars, peering into each one as he passed. The cars seemed to tower high over his head, and to stretch on forever, but finally he came to the car where, he was sure, he had seen someone moving. Again caution told him to be careful, but again, curiosity got the better of him. He reached high over his head, caught the sill of the car, and pulled himself up. Inside, he could see nothing, and he stepped in from the doorway for a better look. *Why didn't I bring a flashlight?* he asked himself reproachfully. He didn't even have a match. He shouldn't—

Behind him the door rumbled shut, and there was a clang of iron as a bolt was latched into place. Outside he could hear a low laugh. He filled his lungs and shouted, "Alan!" There was no answer, only a chuckling sound. "Alan!" He shouted again. "If you're out there, just remember this: I'll get out of this somehow. I'll get out, even if I have to ride all the way to Boston. And I'll come back and find you!" He stopped, waiting to hear the chuckle again, but there was only a faint crunching sound as if someone were walking away up the track.

Very carefully, he felt his way back to the door and ran his hand down it to see if, somehow, he could wedge it open. There was a tiny crack, and he dropped to his hands and knees on the gritty floor, feeling for a loose board, a nail, anything he might use to pry the door open. It took him, he estimated later, half an hour to realize that he was trapped. The floor was clear, and the door was locked. He hammered and screamed until he realized that he was wasting his energy.

Well, maybe the train won't move out of here tonight, he said to himself, and sat down on the floor, his back against the door. Frightened as he was, he finally dozed, until a jolt and a lurch told him that up ahead an engine had been coupled to the boxcars. He stood up and pounded on the door again. "Hey!" he called. "Let me out!" But the only sound he could hear was the faint chuffing of the engine. Then the boxcar lurched again and he was sent reeling across the car. As he grabbed at a crossbeam on the other side, the train started to move, slowly at first, then faster and faster. The boxcar rocked and rolled; it was impossible to stand, so Bert dropped first to his knees, then carefully sat down, bracing himself in the direction the train was racing. A fine shower of cinders and soot drifted in through the crack in the door. Sleep was almost impossible; but somehow Bert dozed again, his palms braced on the floor of the car.

It must have been hours later—Bert had lost track of time, and had forgotten his wrist watch—when the train ground to a stop again and Bert woke from his sleep. His legs ached as he got to his feet. For a moment he listened. Were those footsteps he could hear coming closer?

"Hey!" he called, and hammered again on the door of the car. "Help! In here!" Outside there was the glint of a flashlight, a rattling sound as the lock was released, and then the welcome rumble of the door being rolled back. In the moonlit darkness, a figure was standing. The flashlight blinked off, and Bert looked down into Red Smith's face. He noticed that Red had a finger to his lips.

"Shh!" Red whispered. "I'm not supposed to ride this train." He stretched out his arms. "Here, jump," he said, and Bert stepped off the edge of the car and into Red's grasp. He slid to the ground and stood looking up at Red, who still had his finger to his lips. As Red turned and started down toward the end of the train, Bert did too. They made a wide circle around the caboose where a brakeman was drowsing, and crossed the double tracks. To their right, a short distance up the line, was a railroad station. Just ahead of them was a concrete road, separated from them by a fence.

"Come on," said Red, and bent down to lift up the lowest strand of barbed wire. Bert crawled through, with Red following. They scrambled across a ditch and up onto the paved road.

"I don't know how you got here," Bert said as they walked along side by side, "but I'm certainly glad you did. Where was this train going anyway?"

"To Montreal," Red answered him. "We just branched off from the main line a few miles down."

"But how'd you happen to get aboard?" Bert persisted. "The last I saw of you, you were getting ready to go to sleep."

"That's right," said Red, passing a reflective hand across the stubble on his face. "But just as I was dozing off, I thought I heard someone yelling and pounding. I went back to sleep again, and then I heard the engine coupled on. I don't know, I guess it was just a hunch, but I decided to take a run up to see what was going on. I heard you yell, and just then the train started. So I swung aboard, and decided I'd check up when we stopped again."

"Well, if you hadn't, I'd probably be well on my way to Montreal by now," Bert said gratefully. "Don't know how I ever can thank you."

"Don't try to," said Red. "Just don't ever do anything foolish like that again."

They had approached the railroad station, which lay dim in the blackness, when suddenly its lights went on.

"Must be a passenger train coming," said Red. "Let's go in and see."

The sleepy ticket agent inside told them that a train would be through in a few minutes.

"How far am I from Midvale?" demanded Bert.

"That's my home town."

"Oh, about two hours' trip," said the agent, and he named the fare.

Bert shoved his hand into his pocket and came out with an assortment of change. He painfully counted it, and as he finished, his heart sank. He was forty cents short.

As he puzzled over what to do, he felt Red's hand on his shoulder, and Red's other hand was dropping a quarter, a nickel, and a dime into his palm.

"That makes it," said his friend, "and now I'm off again. So long, boy, and good luck. I'll be seeing you, some day." He turned and went out the door. Bert was about to follow him and say thanks when he heard the shrill whistle of the approaching train.

"Better give me a ticket," he said to the agent, who handed him a precious piece of cardboard. He swung aboard, helped up the steps by a conductor who raised his eyebrows at the sight of the young traveler at this late hour. Then he settled down in a seat and dozed until someone shook him and called, almost in his ear, "Midvale! Midvale!" He scurried groggily off the car and started home on the run. The church clock said 4:00 a.m., and the sky was already beginning to gray with the false dawn.

"I'll tell them about it in the morning," he said to himself as he walked cautiously up to the front steps. He sat down, carefully removed his shoes, and tiptoed back over the same route he had taken some five hours earlier. Howard was still sleeping soundly. Bert gingerly swung himself into bed, closed his eyes, and was asleep almost immediately. He knew he would be tired in the morning, and he wanted all the rest he could get.

CHAPTER FOUR

A TELEGRAM AND TROUBLE

"Daylight in the swamp! Roll out, you lumber-jacks!" This loud yell waked Bert a moment, or so it seemed, after he had dropped off to sleep. As he drowsily shook his head, someone leaned over his bed, and the window shade flew up with a rattling noise. The sun, shining in, hit him in the eyes like a hammer blow, and he squinted as he opened both eyes. Ed was standing beside the bed, looking down at him, a grin on his face.

"Train leaves at nine-thirty, bud," he said, "and here you are, still sleeping at eight-fifteen. Don't you think you'd better get up?" Bert massed the two pillows behind him and sat upright, staring reproachfully at his older brother. He was wide awake now, but still tired, oh, so tired.

"And why didn't you wake me earlier?" he asked truculently.

"That's easy to answer," said Ed, grinning a little wryly. "All I had to do was to take a look at your shoes, and I knew you needed sleep."

Bert glanced at his shoes, left just where he had dropped them, and separated from each other by a distance of five feet. "Oh—oh," he said softly. Even from the bed, he could see the mud and cinders that crusted the sides of the soles.

"That's right," Ed remarked, flopping into a chair. "The cinders tipped me off. Now, where were you? And when did you get back?"

"Well, I was going to tell you and Howie when I got up," Bert said. "The best thing I can say is that I made a fool of myself." Very slowly, he recited the story of his involuntary trip on the freight train. He observed, with some relish, that Ed's blue eyes widened as he told how he had been locked into a car and left to be carried away like so much lumber.

"That's Alan, all right," the older brother said when Bert finished. "And it begins to look as if both the Wallaces mean business. All I can hope is that they don't know where we're going. If they do—" He shook his head ruefully.

Bert put out one hand and touched his brother on the elbow. "Even if they do know, which I doubt, we can still beat 'em," he said reassuringly. "What happened in Utah proved that."

"Maybe so," Ed said thoughtfully, "but I just hope they don't spoil our trip. I've got my mouth all fixed for some of those brook trout and landlocked salmon. It's pretty hard to cast a dry fly when you're worried about somebody sneaking around in the brush."

"Well, my mouth's fixed for some bacon and eggs,' said Bert briskly, stretching his legs to the floor. He made a dash for the bathroom, noting that Howard was already up and out. He scrubbed his face vigorously, as if he were trying to get rid of the freckles, and then threw on a shirt and tweed suit.

"Might as well carry some of this stuff downstairs," he said, and bent down to lift up one of the packs, from which a broad tumpline trailed. He grunted involuntarily as he felt the weight, then raised it to his shoulders and flipped the tumpline up to his forehead.

"Is this the way?" he asked Ed cheerfully. He took a step forward, then reeled backward and sat plump on the floor. The crash, he thought, must have rattled the dishes in the dining-room below. Ed doubled up with laughter and sat down on the bed.

"No," he finally said between bursts of chuckling, "that's not right. You've got to lean *in* to the tumpline with your neck muscles and head. Don't let it pull you backward." He stood up and helped lift Bert to his feet. "Now try it again." Bert bent his head forward against the weight of the pack. He could feel the strain all the way down to his shoulders, but he was able to walk forward, out the door, and, with some clutching at the banisters, down the stairs and into the dining-room. Howard, busy eating his breakfast, stared at him wide-eyed.

"That's Not Right!" Ed Laughed

"You're making a lot of fuss for such a light pack," he said innocently as Bert collapsed against the wall and let the tumpline drop from his forehead and the shoulder straps from his back. The pack dropped, with a hollow thud, to the floor.

"Well, you try it and see how easy it is," said Bert, feeling the drops of perspiration on his forehead. "It's going to take a week to get used to loads like that."

Howard, unaccountably amused, bent over his plate again and then looked up with a smile. "Maybe the pack isn't loaded quite right," he suggested. "Why not look and see? Ed tells me the heaviest objects should be at the bottom; maybe they're at the top in this pack."

Bert grumblingly bent over and loosened the straps that held the contents of the pack in place. Wide-eyed, he looked inside; then looked again, as if he couldn't believe the evidence before him. Howard, watching, let out a whoop.

"Fooled you again!" he said, and brought his hand down on the table so hard that the dishes rattled.

Bert bent down again and, with both hands, lifted a chunk of fireplace wood from the pack. "No wonder," he said musingly. "No wonder it seemed so awfully heavy. Howie, you ought to be ashamed of yourself, playing jokes on a poor old man like me."

Bert sat down to his breakfast, and had barely finished drinking his milk when there was the sound of an automobile horn outside. Through the window, he could see the family car with his father at the wheel.

"Time to go," he announced, and he and Howard got up from the table at the same moment. Ed was already carrying duffle bags, packs, and suitcases down the front walk. With all three boys at work, it took only a moment to load the trunk of the car, to run back for their farewells to their mother, and to jump in the car and slam the doors.

At the station, Constable Brown was lounging ostentatiously against the wall, and Mr. Howland, the agent, was peering out through the window. As Bert walked through, carrying a pack, the Constable gave him a reassuring wink, and then a wave of the hand. This, Bert assumed, meant that Mr. Brown had seen no recent trace of either of the Wallaces.

There was a shrill hoot of a whistle, a grinding of wheels, and a puffing locomotive appeared in sight around the curve. In a moment the train had ground to a stop.

" 'By, Dad," said Bert, and gravely shook hands with his father. The other boys followed suit.

Mr. Walton nodded to the conductor. "Take good care of these boys, Bill," he said to the man in blue. "See that the three of them make the change all right at Potter's Falls."

"You bet I will, Sid," the conductor answered. "We're right on time, too. We'll make connections up the line, and they'll be at—where're they going? Oh, Seboomook! They'll be at Seboomook by five this afternoon. That ought to give them time to get at least a little way up the lake." He looked around to see that all the other passengers were aboard, and let out a roar: "BOOOARD!" The train whistle began to shriek, and Bert and his brothers hurried up the iron steps. Inside, they found seats and settled down to enjoy the trip.

Perhaps an hour or two later, Bert wasn't sure of the exact time, he woke from a doze to feel the train slowing down for another stop. Outside the window he could see a fairly large city, and then the train drew into the station. It was Manchester.

The conductor, hurrying by, stopped long enough to say, "We'll be here fifteen minutes, boys, if you want to stretch your legs."

Bert politely said, "Thank you," but his two sleepy brothers, who wanted to do nothing more than stay where they were, shut their eyes again and ignored the invitation. Picking his way carefully over their legs, Bert walked swiftly down the car and out onto the red brick platform. He was standing there indecisively, wondering whether to go inside and get himself a soda, when he noticed a telegraph messenger running down the platform.

I don't know whether that's for us, or not, he thought to himself, *but it won't hurt to ask. Maybe they've located the Wallaces.* He held up his right arm. "Hey, boy!" he called.

The messenger, a ruddy-faced youngster, came running over to him. "That telegram for Walton?" Bert asked.

"Yup, that's right," said the messenger. "It's addressed to the Walton boys, care of this train. You one of them?"

"I am," Bert assured him, holding out his hand for the message. The messenger thrust a slip of paper at him, and he carefully signed his name. Then he tore open the crisp, yellow envelope and unfolded the message inside. What it said sent a chill down his spine. It had been sent from some little town between Midvale and Manchester, and what it said was: HAVE NICE TRIP STOP WILL SEE YOU SOON STOP DOESN'T MATTER WHETHER YOU GO DOWN SEBOOMOOK OR SOMEWHERE ELSE STOP WILL BE AROUND, LOOKING FORWARD TO NICE VISIT. It was signed by *Alan Wallace.*

With the telegram in his numbed hand, after having read it twice, Bert climbed into the train again. His brothers still were asleep. He debated whether to wake them, and finally decided he would. By dint of much shaking, he persuaded both of them to open their eyes.

"Look here!" he said, and thrust the telegram in front of them. Howard let out a shrill whistle and sat popeyed in his seat. Ed turned a dull red.

"I wouldn't have believed it," Ed said. "How do you suppose they knew where we were going? The station agent didn't tell them. I don't think they saw us get on the train. I can't figure it out."

"Well, I can," said Bert. "That first evening, when we were sitting there with the travel folders, old man Wallace was hiding out on the porch. The windows were open. All he had to do was to listen carefully, and he'd know."

"Maybe we ought to cancel our trip," Howard suggested timidly. Bert wheeled on him, really angry for the first time. His face was almost as red as his hair.

"Cancel? Not on your life! We decided to make this trip, and we're going through with it. Nobody, not even the Wallaces, can stop us!"

"I'm with you, Bert," Ed agreed. "We'll see this thing through and we'll win. They couldn't beat us before, and they can't beat us now!"

CHAPTER FIVE

SABOTAGE

The train from the Junction to Seboomook was a tiny little affair, with an engine that belched smoke and chugged like one of the toys Bert had had a few years ago. In a way, though, the trip was a thrilling one. Almost immediately after leaving the Junction, the train plunged into deep forest. Spruce shaped like church spires; balsam the size of mammoth Christmas trees, and occasionally, Norway pine, with red bark and tall, shaftlike trunks crowned by a tuft of green, crowded down to the tracks on either side. Occasionally there was a tiny lake, the color of the smiling blue sky, alongside the little ribbon of steel. It was like a journey to the end of the world, and all three boys sat with their noses pressed against the grimy windowpane.

Finally, an hour or so later, the train slackened speed, and the conductor strolled into the car. "End of the line, boys," he said. "This is Seboomook."

Outside the windows, the scattered buildings of a tiny settlement were visible, and beyond them the glittering waters of a lake. Loaded with packs, duffle bags, and suitcases, Bert led his brothers down the steps and out onto the station platform.

"Look!" he shouted, and pointed toward the lake. A narrow bay, flanked by pine trees, led out into a broad expanse of a lake dotted with islands. A light breeze was blowing, and little whitecaps rolled in toward a sandy beach along which the village was strung. Seboomook itself seemed to consist of not much more than a general store, the station, and a few houses. Three or four men dressed in identical woods costume of felt hat, checkered shirt and stagged trousers, leaned against the buildings. There was perhaps a block of cement sidewalk, and then the village dwindled into pasture land and clusters of trees.

"Now let's find the canoe!" Bert said happily. "Have you got the receipt, Ed?"

His older brother reached into his pocket and pulled out a glittering metal clip which held together a collection of five-dollar bills and one or two pieces of yellowish paper.

"Sure," he said, removing one of these slips, "here it is. Let's find the station agent and see about it."

The station agent strolled up at that very moment and Ed handed him the slip.

"Yup," he said, "she's down on the platform at the freight house, right down there." He made a vague gesture toward a shanty-like building a short distance away. Dropping their loads, the boys sprinted down to the freight house. The canoe, glittering and trim, had been turned so that its bottom side was uppermost. Bert ran his hands over the gleaming rivets, noted the skillful craftsmanship, and then gently turned it over so that the inside was visible. The newly-varnished paddles had been strapped to the thwarts.

"Let's take it down and put it in the pond and paddle around for a minute!" Bert suggested.

"Okay," Ed agreed. Seemingly without effort, he crouched, lifted the front of the canoe, heaved it on his shoulders; and made his way down to the pond, where he reversed the position of the canoe and slid it gently into the water. Bert was about to jump in the bow, which was on dry land, when Ed stopped him. "You should remember that, Bert. Never step in any part of a canoe that isn't in the water."

"Why?" asked Bert. "Won't it stand my weight?"

"Yes," said his brother, "but these canoes are made of the thinnest possible metal, for lightness. To step into one would bend it. In a wooden canoe, you might break out some of the supports." He lightly stepped onto a flat stone and then into the back of the canoe and busied himself unstrapping the paddles. Then he drew the canoe a short distance up the pond to a tiny dock, and the other two boys got in. Howard sat in the middle; Bert, in the stern with the other paddle.

"She handles wonderfully!" Bert cried, and, indeed, the metal canoe did. It was responsive, easy to maneuver, and fast. With long, dipping strokes, Bert and Ed propelled the canoe from end to end of the pond, and then brought her back to the dock again.

"What a trip we're going to have!" said Bert, who could hardly wait to get started. He helped pull the canoe out on shore.

"Now," Ed suggested, "you take it easy while Howie and I go up to the store and get the rest of our supplies. We've got plenty of dehydrated vegetables and some canned stuff, but we need bacon, eggs, bread, and some smaller items. You can stay here and satisfy your curiosity about the way this canoe is made."

Bert watched his two brothers trudging up the beach to the main street. As soon as they were out of sight, he deftly flipped the canoe over and began to inspect its craftsmanship. He had always been interested in welding and riveting. He ran his hand along the rivets again. One of them seemed to vibrate a little under the pressure of his fingers. *That's funny,* he said to himself, and pressed the rivet between his thumb and forefinger. *I could almost lift it out,* he thought. He gave a sharp twist, and it came loose in his hand. The inner side fell away into the bottom of the canoe with a tinkling sound, leaving a hole through which water could pour. Again Bert felt the same chilly sensation he always associated with the Wallaces.

Somebody's been tinkering with this canoe! he said to himself. He inspected the rivet in his hand. It had been sawed neatly through, and then stuck together again with some sort of solder. Quickly, he began to check the other rivets. Three more of them were loose. With his knuckles, he tapped the air compartments on either end. Then he bent down to examine the outer skin of the canoe at bow and stern. There was a dull patch on the metal, and he felt a roughness under his fingertips. He put his face close to the canoe. Sure enough, both air compartments had been punctured, and then soldered again! The canoe would have held together just long enough for them to get out of sight of shore, and then it would have sunk without a trace! Bert's first impulse was to run up to the store and get his brothers. But, instead of heading for the store, he walked up the beach, digging his toes in the sand, and climbed the steps to the station. The agent was busy at his desk making out waybills. Bert coughed to attract his attention.

"Say," he began, "somebody's been tinkering with our canoe. Sawed some rivets through, and then soldered them back together again. You seen anybody around who might have fooled with it?"

"Why, sonny," said the station agent, a skeptical

look on his face, "everybody in this settlement has been down to look at that canoe at one time or another. But in the daytime, anyhow, there ain't any strangers around. At night there's nobody in the neighborhood of the freight house, and I s'pose a stranger *could* get at it."

"Thanks," Bert flung back over his shoulder as he walked out the door and up the dusty street to the general store. Through its windows, he could see Ed and Howie, with a pile of groceries on the counter in front of them. The storekeeper, a wispy old man, glanced up at him as he entered. Off in the back of the store, a motherly-looking old lady was busy putting boxes into the basket she carried on her arm.

"Somebody's been fooling with the canoe!" Bert gasped. Both his brothers stared at him, doubtfully.

"That's right!" he insisted. He dug in his pocket and pulled out a rivet. "Look at this! Sawed clean through and then soldered together again so it would hold just long enough for us to get out on the lake. If we hit a storm, we'd sink without a trace!"

"That's the Wallaces again," Ed said slowly, bitterly. "But I didn't think they'd stoop to any trick as low as that." He listened, and his face grew grim, as Bert explained hastily how the air compartments had been punctured and then soldered shut again.

"I asked the station agent," Bert concluded, automatically smoothing down his bristling hair, "and he said he hadn't seen anybody around there."

"But I did," came a voice from the back of the store, and the elderly woman came forward. "I'm Mrs. Jones," she introduced herself, "and I live in the farmhouse just across the brook from the freight house.

"Just yesterday I saw a stranger fooling around that canoe of yours. And last night I woke up, couldn't sleep. I looked out the window, and I saw a light over by the station house. I thought it might be burglars, but I knew there was nothing for them to steal except your canoe. I looked a little more carefully, and there were two men there. They seemed to be bending over the canoe, and I could hear a clinking sound, and then a noise like a saw cutting through metal.

"I waked Mr. Jones, and told him to look out the window. He didn't want to get up, but he finally did. 'Don't see a thing,' he told me. 'You must be dreamin'.' So I went and looked again, and there was nobody there. I thought maybe I *was* dreaming, but what you boys have to say makes me sure I *did* see someone."

"Well, that's the Wallaces, all right," Bert said angrily. "And now, what are we going to do? We'll have to take the canoe back to Bangor to get it welded."

"Oh, no, you won't," broke in Mrs. Jones, her face wreathed in a smile. "It just so happens that my boy was a welder in the army. He brought some equipment back with him, and he bought some more, and he's dyin' to get a chance to practice on something."

"Gee, that's wonderful!" Bert said. "We'll take the canoe up to the house right now. Come on, boys, let's go!" With a whoop, he burst out the door, his brothers following.

Down by the water's edge, Bert strapped the paddles back on the canoe and then, emulating his brother, tried to lift it to his shoulders. He stood stiff-legged over the bow of the canoe and tugged and grunted. But as he pulled it toward him, he lost his balance and went sprawling in the sand.

"Use a little economy of motion," Ed said to him. "Watch this." His older brother dropped to a crouching position, his back toward the canoe, and lifted the bow until it was over his head. Then he sidled backward until he was in position, and rose easily to his feet. "That's all it takes," he said, his voice echoing hollowly. "It's always easier to lift a load from a crouching position than it is when you're standing upright." With Bert and Howard trailing him, he started up the winding path toward the little cottage with green shutters that stood by itself in a clearing. A husky young man stood in the doorway and stared curiously at them.

"Will you do some welding for us?" Bert asked him, explaining his plight.

The veteran's face lit up. "Will I!" he said. "I'll do the best welding job you ever saw! You won't be able to sink this boat with a ton of cement when I get done with it!"

CHAPTER SIX

A WARNING SHOT

Before the noise had died away, Bert was out of bed and peering from the window of his tiny room to see what could possibly be making such a racket. On the lawn below, a youngster his own age, in a flaming red shirt, was swinging an ax against a mammoth metal triangle. The sound echoed and boomed against the ancient wooden building; it almost drowned the noise of running feet in the hallway. As Bert stared out the window, his door was flung open, and Howard looked in.

"Breakfast!" his younger brother sang out. "Come and get it!"

Bert jumped quickly into his clothes and sprinted downstairs, across a creaky hallway, and into the dining-room. There, a dozen men in shirtsleeves, their faces tanned from long exposure to the out-of-doors, were busy eating breakfast. Two platters, one piled high with flapjacks, the other with gold and white fried eggs, passed swiftly up and down the table. Bert stuck out his hand as each of them came by; then he spread butter on his flapjacks, poured some maple syrup over them, and began to eat. He old himself he had never been so hungry.

Across the table, Ed looked up from his food and remarked genially, "Boy, from the way we're all eating, I'm beginning to wonder if I guessed wrong on the supplies for the trip. You'd better make good on those fish stories of yours, Bert. We're depending on you to keep the larder filled."

"Well, if the trout and landlocked salmon up here don't object to the flies I've brought along," Bert said, "I don't think we'll have to worry. I want to get enough for us to eat; and I'd also like to get enough big ones so that I can pick out one fish and take him home to be stuffed and mounted to hang on the wall in my room."

"Ha!" came a snort from Howard, who was sitting a little way down the table. "He thinks *he's* going to get the record fish. He doesn't know that I'm going to get him."

"How big is your fish going to be, bud?" Bert demanded, with a mock gruffness in his voice.

"Oh, like *that*," said Howard, flinging out his arms to indicate a fish some three feet long.

"Better watch out, sonny, or he'll drag you right down to the bottom with him," chuckled a sandy-haired man in his middle forties, who was sitting to the left of Howard, and who had dodged the younger brother's outstretched arms just in time.

"I'm Jed Thomas," he said without further pre-

liminaries. "One of the guides up here. You goin'
up the lake?"

"Yes," replied Bert, and he introduced himself
and his brothers. "How does it look today?"

"Well, it'll be sunny, but there may be some wind
squalls," said Thomas. "Stick pretty close to shore
if the wind comes up, and you'll be all right. I'll be
startin' later in the day, and I'll keep an eye out for
you. You can camp on most any island, if you have
to."

"Swell!" said Bert. He cocked an eye at his brothers, and all three of them pushed back their chairs
and got up from the table. On the front lawn, they
could see the gleaming bottom of their canoe, completely re-welded now, and guaranteed shipshape by
Mrs. Jones's son. He had worked on it until late in
the evening, and then had carried it down to the
little hotel himself.

While Ed lingered to pay the bill, Bert and Howard strolled out on the lawn, where their packs and
duffle bags were piled. The lake was just across the
road. They each lifted an end of the canoe and carried it down to a dock at the water's edge, then
began to tote the equipment for their trip across.
There was an occasional fresh gust of wind, but the
weather was appreciably warmer than it had been
the day before.

"Ouch!" said Howard, suddenly, and dropped his

"I'm Jed Thomas, One of the Guides."

load as he slapped at his neck. While Bert was staring at him, wondering what had happened, he felt a stinging sensation on the back of his own neck. When he drew his hand away, in it were the crushed remains of several tiny flies. Bert stared at his palm, amazed that such small creatures could bite so viciously.

"Black flies botherin' you?" came a voice over his shoulder, and he turned his head to look into Jed Thomas's smiling face.

"If that's what you call 'em," said Bert earnestly, "they certainly are. Will we run into many of them up the lake?"

"Many?" echoed the guide, scratching his head. "You'll run into millions of 'em when you get out of the lake and down the river where the wind can't blow 'em away. We'd hoped that the cool weather would keep 'em away a while longer, but here they are, and there's not much we can do about it."

"Good gravy!" cried Bert, genuinely worried. "We'll be eaten alive! Isn't there anything we can do about 'em?"

"Why, sure," the guide drawled. "Go over to the grocery and get yourself half a dozen bottles of what we call lollacapop. It's awful smelly stuff, and it's greasy, too, but if you spread it on your face, and leave it there, and don't wash too often, the flies keep away from you."

"Gosh, thanks!" Bert said, and he ran back across the street to the general store. He bought a dozen small bottles of lollacapop and stuffed them in his pockets. By the time he had reached the lake shore again, the canoe was in the water, with Ed kneeling inside while Howard handed him the packs and duffle bags. Bert knew that their load included a big, pyramidal tent with a mosquito netting doorway, and he was grateful for this thought, in view of the scourge of flies. He watched as Ed carefully completed the loading, making sure that everything was stored amidships, or toward the stern, so that the bow would ride out of the water. The heavy weight made the canoe ride fairly low, but there still remained perhaps ten inches of clearance between its top edge and the water.

"We may have to bail if it gets too windy," Ed remarked, looking up at Bert, "but we certainly can't sink, not since the air tanks have been repaired." With one hand on each side of the canoe, he carefully crawled to the stern and took his seat. Bert leaped into the bow, and steadied the canoe with his paddle while Howard crawled to a position amidships. Ed gave a shove against the sandy, rippled bottom with his paddle, and the canoe glided out into the lake, where little wavelets were beginning to show the force of the intermittent wind. "We're off!" he said, and Bert dipped his paddle into the water.

They had started their trip at last. As Bert dipped his paddle in far ahead and brought it back alongside, he lost himself for a moment in reverie. *What,* he wondered, *would this trip bring them?* Fun and excitement, certainly. Trouble with the Wallaces, very possibly. But whatever happened, they'd learn from it. *We Waltons always do learn,* he reminded himself.

The pine-clad headlands slid by swiftly, and the village became a lessening dot on the shore line behind them. Bert was beginning to feel an ache in his shoulder muscles. He would have liked to stop paddling, but that would mean that Ed would be carrying the load. What's more, the wind was freshening. As the canoe shot out from the mouth of the narrow bay, and into the main lake, a gust hit them like a blow of a fist. Big whitecaps were rolling up. The sky remained deceptively blue, but it began to look as if trouble were ahead. The shore line, at this point, was composed of high sand bluffs, in places fringed by rocky reefs. No place to land, Bert saw, and no place to get in the lee of the wind. All they could do was to keep paddling.

The waves went slap-slap against the bow of the canoe. Once or twice, a particularly big comber broke, spattering Bert with spray. It was exhilarating, and he turned just long enough to grin at

Ed for a second. Ed was still smiling, but there was
a trace of tightness around his mouth, as if he were
anticipating more trouble to come. Off to their right,
as Bert kept up his paddling, there was a tiny island,
but the foam and spray were shooting high from the
rocks that surrounded it. Perhaps a mile ahead was
a larger island, which looked as if it might have a
little cove where they could find shelter.

"Breakers ahead!" Bert called over his shoulder.
Between strokes of his paddle, he stole a look at Ed.
The grin had vanished from his older brother's face,
and a taut, determined expression had replaced it.
Howard was dozing in his seat amidships; being
down on a level with the water, unable to see ahead,
he couldn't possibly realize that trouble was brewing.
It might be real trouble, Bert told himself. By now,
the wind had risen to a shrill screech, and he could
see the tall pines on shore bending before its blast.
Still, the shore line led along parallel to the force of
the wind, and there was no place to take shelter.

The canoe cut cleanly through each wave, but the
interval between waves was lessening a little. Now
the three boys were dipping down into the trough,
then riding high on the spuming crest. It was a
capricious, tricky wind, the kind that would blow
steadily for a minute or two at a time and then re-
lent. When the wind blew, Bert had to paddle to
keep the canoe from drifting backward. When it let

up for a few seconds, the boys would make progress. The island still seemed tantalizingly far away.

"Look out!" Ed shouted, interrupting Bert's reverie, and Bert looked far ahead to see a mammoth wave, the granddaddy of them all, bearing down on them. Ed was an expert helmsman, and they swung so that they were quartering to the wave. Thus, though they felt its shock, they rode it out, and slid down the slick trough on the far side. Howard, sitting on the bottom of the canoe, was sputtering and thoroughly frightened. An inch or two of water made his perch a cold one, and he began to bail with his cap. Bert only had time to steal a quick glance at poor Howie, but the sight made him whoop with laughter. "Like trying to bail out the ocean with a teaspoon!" he hooted, his words carrying back to Howard on the wings of the wind.

Gradually, painfully, the island was drawing closer. Off to his right, Bert could see a patch of calmer water and what looked like a quiet, restful cove. The thought of being able to release his death grip on the paddle filled him with happiness. His hands felt as if they were afire; his shoulders were stinging from the concentrated effort he had made. He looked at his watch. They had been under way for two hours, and still they could vaguely see the village down the bay behind them. *At this rate, it'll take a year to make the trip we've planned*, he said grimly to himself.

Slowly, the canoe swung toward the harborage. Bert felt a thrill of gratitude to Ed—old, reliable Ed —who carefully changed his course, but never enough so that they might be broadside to the waves. Finally, the whitecaps began to dwindle to a long, rolling swell, and then to ripples. Just as the prow of the canoe cut into calm water, Bert heard a shrill noise, like the buzzing of an angry wasp; and then, from shore, the sound of a rifle being fired. He could hardly believe his ears. He strained his eyes toward shore, and finally made out the ugly outline of a rifle, with a man behind it, both of them half concealed in the woods that came down to the sandy shore line. There was another shrill noise and a bang.

"Let's get out of here!" Bert shrieked to his brother in the stern. "They're firing ahead of us. It must be a warning to stay off!" With deep, lunging strokes of the paddle, they swung around, and out again into the full fury of the storm.

The Wallaces again, Bert thought with grim resignation. *But how'd they get ahead of us?* And then he thought, with a sinking feeling, *They're mighty smart. Nobody'll hear rifle fire in this kind of a wind. They wouldn't try to shoot directly at us; that would be too obvious. No, they'll just drive us out into the lake and hope that we get swamped.*

Far ahead, through the welter of wind and foam
he could see a still tinier island than the one from
which they had been driven. A single pine crowned
a rocky knoll; around it were a few smaller spruce
trees, and then a little pocket handkerchief square
of beach. Grimly, he bent to his paddle, and slowly
the island came closer. At last they were in calm
water again, and then, as they headed for shore, Bert
felt an ugly grating against the bottom of the canoe.
"Back paddle!" he yelled to his older brother. Un
derneath them were needle-sharp rocks and wide
fanged boulders which could rip the silvery hide of
their canoe apart in a second. Bert was sick with dis
appointment. He rested on his arms, breathing in
great gulps of air, and waiting for Ed to suggest
something.

"All we can do is to cruise around the island, far
enough off so that we won't go aground," his broth
er's voice carried forward to him. "Maybe there's
another cove we can get into."

With a sinking feeling, Bert dipped his paddle in
the water again, and they shot out into the cross
chop at the corner of the island. As they came out
of the lee and into the wind, Bert looked ahead. Was
that a tiny channel he saw, winding in between two
spruce trees? It was! He lifted his paddle and used
it as a pointer. A broad grin spread across Ed's face
and he nodded vigorously. It was a delicate opera

tion. They had to come broadside to the waves, and then run crosswise to the wind. Ed handled his paddle masterfully. All Bert had to do was to keep paddling. Afterward, rubbing his sore muscles, he wondered how he'd done it. They were rocking in the trough of the waves, which seemed to tower high over them.

"Now," Ed shouted. Bert lunged with his paddle and took six deep strokes. Then they were flying into the quiet of a tiny little cove, where the trees hung over the water, and the pebbly bottom of the lake was plainly visible through a great depth of water. Bert sagged forward in his seat. He felt as if he could fall asleep right there, but Ed's reassuring voice brought him back to consciousness.

"Let's get ashore," said his older brother. "It's going to be a clear night, so we won't pitch the tent, but we ought to get some food into ourselves."

The canoe grated on a sandy beach and Bert, stretching his stiffened legs, stepped out onto a shore he had never expected to feel again beneath his feet. He pulled the canoe a little way up on the beach, and then sat down weakly in the sand. Howard jumped out swiftly, and then Ed stepped into the water and waded ashore.

"Howie, get a fire going," Ed snapped, and the youngest brother scurried off into the trees, returning a few minutes later with an ample supply of dried branches and even a small log or two. Soon, the aromatic smell of burning wood was drifting up through the trees into the windy heavens. In the cove it was as calm as though no wind was blowing, even though Bert could hear it whistling overhead. Numbly, he helped unpack the food.

"Frankly, I'd rather sleep," he mumbled to Ed. "I don't feel like eating."

"And that's the very time you *have* to eat," his older brother chided him. "You must never feel too tired to take some food into your system. You'll need it tomorrow to keep going." And, as Bert spooned up the corned beef hash that Howard had swiftly prepared, and took a sip of steaming cocoa, he agreed that food wasn't too bad an idea at that point.

CHAPTER SEVEN

MAROONED

Of all things in the world that Bert wanted to do, he wanted to sleep. He was desperately tired. He leaned back against a massive, water-polished boulder, and fell into a doze before he knew it. As he closed his eyes the sun was sinking behind the spiky pine trees far off on the shore line, and Mt. Katahdin, remote in the distance, was outlined with a red glow that silhouetted its crag and granite walls. It seemed only a moment later when he was roughly awakened. He glanced up to see Ed, a half-smile on his face, and then swiftly realized that he had slept for some time. The long, northern dusk had begun. The shore line was just dimly visible, and a little cap of clouds lay over the hills just behind it.

"Good gravy!" he said. "I must have been awfully tired. Seems like just a minute since I went to sleep."

"I know," Ed answered him, "and I'd have liked to let you sleep there all night, except that you'd have been awfully stiff in the morning. The thing is, we've got to cut some boughs and make ourselves some proper beds. Then we can sleep late in the morning. Okay?"

Bert managed a grin as he stumbled to his feet. His shoulder muscles ached dully, and even his face seemed stiff, somehow. All around him, the little balsams crowded in. With a sureness born of long experience, he picked up an ax and began to clip large branches from the feathery trees. He didn't need to be told which trees were balsam and which were spruce. When he was much younger, he had ignored the flat needles that distinguish a balsam and had proudly made himself a bed from the prickly branches of the spruce. The discomfort he suffered that night taught him a lesson he never forgot. Now he chose his balsam discriminatingly, and with a thought for the next passer-by. Where some careless woodsmen will chop down a young tree and strip it bare, because it is less effort, he took just a few branches from each tree, and those were low-lying. Now and then he would cast a quick glance at the tree he was pruning to make sure that he hadn't taken too many branches. As he accumulated a pile, he thatched these neatly on the handle of his ax and carried them back to a flat spot which Ed had selected as the night's campground. Ed was also cutting balsam boughs, and Howard was preparing the bed.

"That's the way to do it," Ed said encouragingly as he looked down at Howard's work. The younger brother had stripped each small branch from the larger ones. He was shoving them into the ground, butt down, so that the balsam made a deep, springy carpet. It took more than an hour to make a good bed, and then Howard called out, "Come and try it now, and see what you think!"

Bert willingly set down his ax, making sure that it was in a place where he could find it easily in the morning, and stretched out on the fragrant branches with a luxurious sigh.

"Feels swell," he said approvingly. "Just like an innerspring mattress." Howard accepted the compliment graciously and then began to unstrap one of the duffle bags. From its capacious interior, he pulled out three eiderdown sleeping bags, each neatly rolled and tied, and flung them over on the balsam bed. Bert grabbed his own bag, sat up to unlace his shoes, and started to set them to one side when he was struck with a sudden thought. He reached a hand in his pocket and came out with a length of cord, which he stretched between two of the larger trees.

"What's the idea?" Howard asked him. "Planning to wash some clothes, or what?"

"Simple," said Bert. "There're bound to be porcupines on this island, and there's nothing they like better than a little leather, or anything with perspiration in it. I'm going to hang my shoes from this line, and then the porkies can't get at them." He suited his action to the word as Howard looked on skeptically.

"Better do the same thing," Bert suggested to his younger brother. "Otherwise, you may have to finish the trip barefooted."

"Aw, I'll keep 'em right alongside me," said Howard. "I'm not so sure there are porcupines here, anyway."

"Well, suit yourself," said Bert, patiently. "I just hope one of us wakes up in time if a porky comes along." He stripped off his outer clothes, extracted a pair of light pajamas from a pack, slipped into them and then stuck his feet into his sleeping bag. It was cold, and the first chill struck through to his bones; but, in a moment, he began to feel the warmth of the eiderdown. He had not bothered with a pillow; as tired as he was, he didn't need one. He turned on his stomach and fell asleep almost immediately.

Thump! came a sound. *Thump! Thump!* Bert drowsily shook his head and sat up in his sleeping bag. By now, it was midnight according to the illuminated hands of his wrist watch. Across the lake, the fog hung lower on the mountains. The silver crescent of a waning moon sent a glitter of light across the waters of the lake. The wind had subsided, and there was scarcely a sound to be heard but the thumping.

"What in the dickens can it be?" Bert asked himself. He was still only half awake. Suddenly, he stiffened. Could somebody be tampering with their canoe? Could it be the Wallaces? Cautiously, he crawled out of his sleeping bag and got to his feet, holding the sleeping bag so that it draped over his shoulders. He stuck one arm outside and felt the chill of a Maine night. At his side he had carefully placed a flashlight. He bent down and picked it up, but did not try to turn it on. In a pinch it was heavy enough to be used in self-defense. Gradually his eyes became accustomed to the darkness.

Thump! there was the noise again. Just beyond Howard he could see a dark figure, not very big. *A porcupine!* he said to himself. *And he's after Howie's shoes!* Very slowly, he picked up a heavy chunk of wood that lay just to the left of the balsam bed. Howard still slept peacefully. Bert took careful aim. *Bang!* The stick landed squarely on the surprised porcupine. There was an outraged yap; at the same moment Howard seemed to leap out of his sleeping bag, his tow-colored hair bristling and his eyes round with alarm.

"Porcupine," said Bert briefly. "He was trying to get away with one of your shoes." He clicked on the flashlight. In its beam, on the edge of the tiny clearing, he could see the porcupine, its brown quills tipped by a touch of white, bristling with surprise and anger. "Scat!" he said aloud, and heaved another chunk of wood at the animal. It retreated at a dignified pace into the woods.

"Does that convince you?" Bert asked his wide-awake younger brother. There was no sarcasm in his voice, only a note of inquiry.

"You bet!" said Howard. "I'll hang those shoes up right now." He looked quickly at Ed. "Still sleeping," he said in a whisper, and put a finger to his lips. Then, as Bert watched, he extricated himself from the sleeping bag, tiptoed barefoot to the line Bert had strung, and carefully hung up his shoes. Bert sighed, lay down, and settled back into his warm bag. Still, the porcupine wouldn't let him sleep. Angry and noisy, the animal had climbed ponderously into a tree, where it alternated yapping with a clicking of its teeth. *Almost as if it had false teeth,* Bert thought as he lay there sleepless.

At one point, however, the porcupine must have decided it was a useless job. There was silence, and it lasted long enough for Bert to drop off into a sleep of exhaustion. By now, he was so tired that he was beginning to have nightmares. Strangers stalked through his dreams; once or twice he awoke to the soundlessness of the night. The last time he woke, he thought he heard a grating sound. *That porcupine again!* he said to himself, and promptly dropped off to sleep.

It was bright daylight when he awoke. A fire was

crackling briskly on a rock just a few feet in front of the bough bed, and there was the cheerful rattle of a frying pan, from which drifted the smell of frying bacon. Bert yawned luxuriously and stuck his head out of the sleeping bag. He consulted his watch. It was eight o'clock!

"Time to get up!" Ed called to him from the fire. "We've got pancakes and bacon this morning. And somewhere, we've got some syrup. I haven't been able to find it yet."

Bert crawled from the bag and darted down to the water to wash his face. The canoe had been left just around the bend. For a moment, Bert thought he ought to reassure himself that it was still there. "I'll check on it the first thing after breakfast," he remarked. He sprinted back to the fire, warmed himself for a second, and then slipped into the clothes he had worn the day before, plus a comfortable pair of moccasins.

"Here you go," Ed said to him, handing him a plate stacked with pancakes. Two crisp strips of bacon were draped over the top. Bert snatched up a knife and fork from the pile of utensils stacked alongside the fire, and got ready to dig in.

"But where's the syrup?" he demanded. "Can't eat this without syrup."

"Gosh, for a moment I forgot," Ed said, looking quickly around him at the pile of packs and duffle bags. "Say, did either of you bring up that littlest pack from the canoe?" The three boys looked blankly at one another.

"I'll bet I forgot it," Howard said, putting down his plate. "I'll go get it."

Bert began to nibble meditatively on a strip of bacon, and broke off a chunk of pancake. It was light and feathery, he decided, but it didn't taste right without syrup. In the underbrush, he could hear Howard crashing down toward the canoe. A minute later, there came a yell from Howard.

"Hey! Come here!" the younger brother shouted. There was something compelling in the yell. Bert set down his plate with a clatter and started for the canoe on the run. He burst through the fringe of overhanging branches along the cove, and stopped short on the beach. Howard was there, but the canoe was gone! Wavelets lapped up on the sand, and a deep groove showed where the canoe had been drawn up on the shore. Around it were two sets of footprints, one large, one smaller.

"They've done it again!" Bert whispered to himself, feeling a sinking sensation at the pit of his stomach. "They've stolen our canoe!"

"Who, the Wallaces?" asked Howard, astonishment written on his face. "But how could they do it without our hearing them?"

"Heck, there was so much noise from that porcu-

"They've Stolen Our Canoe!"

pine last night that anything could have happened,"
Bert said bitterly. "They'd like to maroon us here.
I'll bet they would have swiped all our food if we
hadn't brought most of it up with us."

He stared out at the blank expanse of the lake.
Not a boat was in sight.

"Well, come on," he finally said. "Let's go back
and tell Ed." He burrowed his way through the
underbrush and walked disconsolately out into the
clearing. The fire was still crackling and snapping
cheerily, and Ed was looking curiously at him as,
with his head down, he strolled over to the fire.

"What's wrong, Bert?" asked his older brother.
"Didn't you find the syrup?"

"Nope," said Bert dourly. "We didn't."

"Did you look all through the canoe?" asked Ed.

"The canoe's gone," said Bert dully. He could
see the look of astonishment on his older brother's
face, a look that all too soon was supplanted by a
dull glow of rage.

"Well," said his older brother, finally controlling
himself, "we still have to eat. After that, we can start
thinking about ways of getting ourselves off this
island. Somebody's bound to come by pretty soon."
He handed Bert a container full of sugar, from
which Bert spooned enough to sweeten the pancakes. By now, these were cold, and each mouthful
took an effort to swallow. The three brothers ate

silently, lost in thought.

"What do you suppose they've done with the canoe?" Howard finally asked as he took a last sip of cocoa and leaned back to consider the prospect.

"Probably towed it out and let it drift ashore somewhere," said Bert. "It may land up in some deserted cove and lie there for weeks before anybody discovers it."

"Well, anyway, we won't starve to death," put in Ed. "Nothing really bad can happen to us. We've got plenty of food, even if we don't have any syrup."

"Yeah, but our trip's delayed," contributed Bert. "They must be hoping we'll get discouraged and turn back. Or else—or else they're planning something worse for us, and want time to get things ready." He sipped down the last scalding gulp of cocoa and then stood up.

"Since we may be here a while," he added, "I'm going to chop some firewood. We might as well lay in a supply." He reached for the ax, which leaned against a rock, and then said angrily, "That porcupine! He's gotten away with the leather cover for the ax. I forgot all about it last night."

"Well, there isn't much area to search," Ed suggested. "Why don't you take a little walk and look for it?"

Bert nodded, grasped the ax, holding it by the handle in his right hand, well away from his side, so that if he tripped and fell the blade wouldn't injure him.

"Okay," he said. "I'll start exploring." He pushed aside the underbrush and, in a second, was out of sight.

The trees seemed to be thicker back here in the woods. They crowded together so closely that Bert could barely wedge them apart. Spiky branches slapped at his face, and prickly needles, dislodged by his passage, began to drop into his open collar. It was hot and windless, and Bert soon was perspiring. Some little distance off, he could catch a glint of blue water, the other side of the island. Ahead of him was a little mound, apparently composed of tiny slivers of rock. He kicked impatiently at one of them and then, as he was climbing more steeply, tripped and fell.

"Ouch!" he said, and lifted his left hand for inspection. There was a tiny scratch on it, from which a little blood was oozing. He looked down to see what had caused it. A sharp fragment of some strange type of rock—or was it rock at all?—had cut him. Very gently, he laid down the ax and reached over to dislodge the fragment.

"Why, it's not rock at all," he said to himself. He rubbed at the fragment.

"It's pottery!" he said. "Dollars to doughnuts, I've found an Indian mound!" He lifted his voice, and in a second could hear Ed and Howard crashing through the underbrush. When they were close enough so that he could see them, he held out the pottery fragment. Without a word, all three boys began to dig at the mound with their bare hands.

"Here's an arrowhead!" called out Howard, holding up a roughly chiseled piece of stone. "And here's the rest of that piece of pottery!" said Ed, his two hands heaped with fragments. The pile of relics grew—arrowheads, pottery, even a bead or two.

"These may be priceless," Bert mused. "Perhaps our bad luck is our good luck, too. Maybe we'll find enough treasure here to pay for our trip!" For the moment, he forgot that they were marooned on the island, but Ed brought him back to reality.

"You keep on digging," said his older brother. "I'm going back to shinny up a tree down on the shore line, and hang out a white shirt. That'll be our distress signal. Maybe, if we're lucky, somebody'll come along before the end of the day and get us out of here."

CHAPTER EIGHT

AN OMINOUS RUMBLE

A silent swarm of black flies, gathering in the stillness of the woods, reminded Bert that he must smear on some fly dope. He took the bottle from his pocket, poured a little of the greasy liquid onto his hands, and smeared it over his face. As if by magic, the flies began to stay away from him, and he continued his work of excavation untroubled. By now he had amassed a huge pile of relics—enough, he told himself, to prove that this was a splendid example of an Indian mound. He sat down for a moment to rest, and then heard a shrill call from the shore.

"Somebody must be in sight!" he told himself, and started at a half-run for the beach. He had not forgotten the ax; he held onto it tightly; and, once or twice, used it to clip a way through the underbrush. He came out on the shore just above the cove, but the beach was broad and hard, and it took him only a moment to round the corner. What he saw was a welcome sight—the broad, mackinaw-clad back of a stranger talking earnestly to Ed and Howard. Bert broke into a run and drew up, panting, alongside the trio.

"Oh, hello!" he shouted, and stuck out his hand. The visitor was Jed Thomas, the guide whom the brothers had met at breakfast down at the village. Thomas gravely shook his hand.

"Been havin' trouble, eh, sonny?" he inquired. His face crinkled into a grin as Bert nodded vehemently.

"Well, I reckon I kin get you out of it," said the guide. "Do you want me to take one of you back to the village, or do you want to look for the canoe? It must be somewhere on the lake, and I think I kin guess about where 'tis."

"Gosh, let's look for the canoe!" said Bert earnestly. "But where is it?"

"That's not too hard to figger out," said the guide, patting the upturned curve of his own canoe. He drew a pipe from his pocket and sat down on the sand to fill and light in. As a cloud of tobacco smoke spread out in the still air, scaring away whatever flies there were, Jed drew a map in the sand with his index finger.

"Here's the east shore of the lake," he said, tracing out the headlands and indentations. "And here's where we are." His fingertip made a dot in the sand.

"Now then," he continued, puffing deeply at his pipe, "the wind was blowin' from nor'-nor'west yestiddy. So if they let your canoe loose to drift, she'd wind up somewhere between here (he scratched a deep line) and here (another line) which is about six miles of shore line."

"But suppose they took it out and sank it somewhere?" asked Bert, striving to keep a note of worry out of his voice. He didn't succeed very well, for the guide looked up at him sharply.

"Well, the wind kept blowin' until early this mornin'," said the guide, "and I very much mistrust that they'd try to carry a load of rocks out into the lake to sink her. More likely, they went into that same area I just showed you. There's plenty of boulders along the shore line. What they didn't realize, mebbe, is that the water in this lake is so clear you look down forty feet."

"Okay," said Bert, enthusiastic by now, and filled with confidence in Jed. "I'll go along, if you want me to go. And Ed, too. Howie, why don't you stay here and get things packed up?" Jed pulled his canoe parallel with a large rock on the shore line, beyond which the water shoaled off to greater depths, and the two boys carefully got in. As the guide paddled out into the main current with sure, long strokes, Bert breathlessly told him about the Indian mound.

"Yup," said the guide, "that's probably another one of them mounds. Scientists all the time are comin' up here from the universities for Indian relics. Pay pretty good for 'em, too. I guess they just never happened to get around to this little vest-pocket island. Well, anyway, I'll tell the sheriff when I get back, and we'll make sure that you're credited with discoverin' the stuff."

Bert solemnly shook hands with Ed, who sat in the middle of the canoe, and then fixed his gaze on the shore line. It hardly seemed possible that the lake could be so calm and that they could be crossing it so quickly. Ahead of them loomed a deep bay, with rocks protruding fang-like from the water at its head.

"Let's look here first," suggested Jed. "It's the most protected of the lot."

Skillfully he sent the canoe darting through a narrow opening in the rocks. On either side, Bert could see huge boulders extending down into the deep green water.

"You boys keep your eyes peeled," Jed's voice drifted forward to them. "This might be the place." Bert strained his eyes and looked down into the water. A pang of disappointment shot through him as they reached the head of the bay and turned to go up the other side.

"Hey, wait a minute!" Ed called, a note of excitement in his voice. "I see something shiny a little way ahead." Jed plunged his paddle into the water and slowed the canoe. Bert peered into the crystalline water. Beyond and below him, he could see a dim outline, gleaming dully. The canoe scarcely moved now.

"That's it!" he finally said. "That's our canoe!" Jed maneuvered so they were directly over the buried canoe. Bert could see that it was piled high with huge boulders. Just inshore was a flat, shelving ledge of rock, on which the Wallaces obviously had stood. On shore was a great boulder bank, from which they had collected all the rock necessary to sink the boat.

"Nice people!" Bert said bitterly. "And now, how do we get her up?"

"You kin swim, can't you, sonny?" Jed asked quietly.

"Why, sure," said Bert, "and so can my brother here. You mean, we'll have to dive for it?"

"That's right," said the guide. "It'll be chilly work. Water's cold. But it'll be fast, too. Every rock you lift out makes the canoe come up higher, that is, if the air chambers haven't been punched through again. Pret' soon, you'll have her afloat, and then we kin lift out the rest of the rocks at leisure." He maneuvered his canoe alongside the ledge, and the two boys stepped out. Bert stripped to his under-clothing, and stuck one bare toe in the water.

"Brr!" he shivered. "Well, here goes!" and he dived in, pulling himself downward with steady, powerful strokes. He just grazed the canoe, and then he had to come up for a breath. He scrambled ashore, rested for a minute in the warm sun, and dived down again. This time, he was able to grasp a rock and pull himself down so his feet were touching bottom. With one swift motion, he lifted the boulder and dropped it over the side of the canoe. As he rose to gulp in more air, Ed's body flashed by him. In relays, they lifted boulders until the canoe began to stir a little. After each trip they rested, for the water was bitterly cold.

"She risin' any?" asked Jed, as Bert came up for another breath of air.

"Yeah," said Bert, and dived again. By now the canoe was rising perceptibly, and the depth of the dives was steadily being reduced. Bert's arms were beginning to feel numb, and he noticed that ⌐d's lips were blue, but they were winning their fight. As he trod water and heaved one more boulder over the edge, the canoe suddenly burst out of the water, and Bert came up to cling on its side.

"Come ashore," called Jed. "We've got her licked!" The guide reached out to bring the canoe alongside the rock, and helped to throw out the last of the boulders. The glittering canoe floated free and buoyant again. Obviously, her air compartments had not been tampered with. Bert, Ed, and Jed lifted her onto the ledge and carefully inspected her. There were a few dents, but the canoe was sound. What was more important, the paddles were still there. They had been wedged under the thwarts and along the sides in such a fashion that they weren't damaged.

"Hop in and try her out," Jed suggested. The two boys climbed in, took a paddle each, and tentatively made a trip around the bay. The canoe handled perfectly, and Bert was grinning happily as they pulled up alongside the ledge again.

"She's okay!" he called out to Jed, who flung him an answering grin. "And it's thanks to you we found her." He reached out a hand and shook Jed's extended hand.

"That's all right, sonny," said the guide. "It was just luck. Now, I'd better get back to the village. I just come up the lake to look in on a camp I own when your brother signaled me. And you go ahead and have a good time. I may see you later, up the river." He nodded, and turned toward his own canoe.

"Thanks!" called Bert. And "Thanks again!" echoed his brother as they started out through the narrow, rocky channel and into the lake.

As Bert and Ed swung into the cove of their own little island, a wide grin split Howard's face, and he jumped up and down on the sand. "Boy, oh boy!" he yelled, unable to restrain himself. "The canoe's all right!"

Bert lifted his paddle as the bow grounded on the sand, and jumped out to slap his brother on the back.

"Sure, we'll go right on now. I see you've got everything loaded up, ready to go."

"Didn't miss a thing," said Howard proudly. "Including this." He held up, for Bert's inspection, the sheath of the ax. "I found it out in the brush a little way. Guess it wasn't tasty enough for the porcupine."

Quickly the boys loaded their supplies, clambered into the canoe, and paddled out through the mouth of the cove. Far off, the shore line seemed to narrow in. "That's where we go," said Bert, pointing with his paddle. "That's the dam. If we're lucky, we ought to catch a trout or two below there."

The wind, which had been on their flank, suddenly switched behind them, and they sped toward the head of the lake, blessed with a following breeze. The shore—in minutes, it seemed, but actually in hours—began to draw in, and they could smell the sweet odor of juniper and the sharper tang of the conifers. Occasionally the line of woods was broken by a clearing and a camp. Ahead, and visible now, was a great wooden framework. Through an opening in its center, the waters cascaded down. Bert had expected a great wave of roaring sound, but he had to stop paddling to hear the low mutter of the waterfall. Ahead and to the right of them, just before the dam, was a long, low dock with a shanty at the top that looked both up the lake and down the stream. A man was sitting there in a rocking chair, puffing away at a pipe. As the canoe drew alongside, he looked down on Bert and the other brothers from his perch and said, "Hi."

"Hi," Bert acknowledged the greeting. "Where do we portage our canoe?"

"Right up past the house here," said the man. "Then it's just a little walk down to below the rapids."

As Bert leaped out and steadied the canoe, the other two boys began to unload their supplies on the rock. The canoe, lightened, steadily rose upward. Finally it was empty. Bert and Ed lifted it from the water and pulled it up on the dock.

"Let's take a run up to talk with this man a minute," Ed suggested. Bert and Howard, grateful for any excuse to delay the tedious job of portaging their supplies, happily agreed. All three of them climbed the steep, dusty path to the porch.

"Sit down," said the pensive man in the rocking chair. "I'm the gatekeeper here at the dam. You goin' on down the river?"

"That's right," Bert said, speaking for his brothers. "How's the fishing?"

"Good, about half a mile below the portage," replied the gatekeeper. "They've been pullin' some big trout out of there. You know about the gates on the dam, here?"

"No," answered Bert, "we don't. What are we supposed to know, anyway?"

"Well, when the gates is open, the river may come up five feet in five minutes," explained the languid gatekeeper. "Then you've got to run fer it."

"Gee, maybe we'd better not fish today." Bert wondered anxiously. "We don't want to get caught."

"Don't worry about it today." The gatekeeper laughed. "I'm not goin' to open the gates. But when you come back, better send someone on ahead before you fish those pools to make sure I'm keepin' the gates shut." Inside his camp, a telephone jangled angrily, and he rose and disappeared from sight.

"Let's get going," suggested Ed, and led the way back to the dock. The portage, as the boys feared, was a little less easy than the gatekeeper had made it appear to be. Once or twice, as they carried the canoe over their heads, they slipped on the boulders and nearly fell. There was a swamp, where the mud sucked at their boots, and a briar patch, where the mosquitoes hummed and buzzed.

It took three trips before everything had been carried over the portage and dropped beside a deep pool through which the water of the rapids, reduced to low speed, ran with visible eddies and currents.

"We're off!" Bert shouted when the canoe was loaded and he dipped his paddle in the water as they shot out into mid-current. The river was widening and shallowing as they dropped downstream. They came to a gentle riffle that dropped into a pool where the sandy bottom was visible through the dark water.

"This must be the place." Bert grinned. "Let's pull ashore and wade in for our fishing. We'll dry out, quickly enough, with all this sun." He had fastened the aluminum case containing his fishing rod under the gunwale of the canoe. It took only a moment to unstrap it, and to extricate the shiny, bamboo rod. Swiftly Bert tied on a shimmering leader, and then, after pondering a minute, a red and yellow streamer, a Mickey Finn.

Howard, who had fished only with bait, watched him interestedly. "What's that supposed to represent?" he asked.

"A minnow," explained Bert. "A trout sees this, and if his appetite is good, he'll gobble it up before he knows that he has a mouthful of hair and feathers."

Bert pulled a length of line out through the ferrules of his rod, and then deftly began to cast into the pool just below the riffle, bringing back the streamer each time with a jerky motion that originated in his wrist. Suddenly, he felt the familiar tug on the line. Automatically he twisted back his wrist, tightening the line and setting the hook. Very carefully, he let the fish run, but not too far then brought him back. This he repeated time and again, waited until he knew the trout was weakening and then with a flip of his wrist threw the fish out on shore. It was a beauty—fourteen inches long, with bronze back and a flaming red belly, so typical of northern trout. Bert bent to his fishing again and moved out farther into the stream.

Somewhere upriver, he could hear a faint rumble. He ignored it, and cast again. The rumble grew a little louder. He was absorbed in trying to reach a calm spot just behind a massive log.

"Bert! Bert, watch out!"

It was Howard calling, and as Bert glanced over his own shoulder, he could see the look of anguish on his younger brother's face. He glanced in the other direction, for just a second, to look at Ed, who was fishing from the shore. The rumbling sound had grown to the volume of a roar, like an immense freight train passing by. Bert suddenly looked upstream. What he saw paralyzed him with fear. Around the bend there swept a tumbling torrent of water, a wall as high as his head. Mammoth boulders were hidden from sight. The torrent compressed itself into a narrow canyon. Then, as Bert started to move toward shore, stumbling and clumsy in waist-deep water, the flood was upon him. He felt himself being tumbled head over heels; his lungs were bursting, and great, red discs whirled in front of his eyes. He was being swept along like a match stick, swept along and pulled down, down into deeper water.

CHAPTER NINE

KIDNAPED

The roar of the waters remained in Bert's ears, but he no longer had to fight for breath. Gasping, he drew in a lungful of air and then expelled it. Merely being able to breathe had never seemed so swect before. Very tentatively he opened his eyes and looked up into the smiling face of his brother, Howard. He was lying on a sand bank, and over his head the great pines spread their branches.

"Howie?" he whispered weakly. His brother put out a hand and touched him on the shoulder. "What happened? Where am I now?"

"You're okay, Bert," his younger brother said huskily. "Just rest a minute."

Bert lay back, looking at the sun that filtered down through the branches, and then pushed himself up so that he was leaning on his elbows. Off to his left, the waters still roared. He could see the spray flying high in the air; out over the stream the sun shone through the misty particles and made a tiny rainbow. Very weakly, and with Howard's hand supporting him, he got to his feet and looked around.

"Wow, but that was close!" His younger brother grinned. "I didn't think I could get to you in time."

"How did you do it?" Bert asked. He felt a little shaky and sat down for a moment on a projecting tree trunk.

"Why, when I saw you lose your balance, I lit out on a run," explained Howard. "There was a path through the woods that looked like a cutoff. I saved about a quarter of a mile of stream by taking it. Just as I got there, I saw the current carrying you in toward shore. I dived in, grabbed you, swam with the current, and came out on this sand bank a little farther downstream."

"That was wonderful." Bert smiled. "Howie, you saved my life."

"Yeah," said his brother, with an impish grin, "but I didn't save your fishing pole. That's halfway to who-knows-where by now."

"Who cares about a fishing pole?" demanded Bert. "I can always borrow Ed's. And, by the way, where *is* Ed?"

Bert slowly got to his feet. His clothes were still sodden and dripping, and there was a pool of water in each of his shoes. He had never before come quite so close to death, and the level-headedness of Howie was all that saved him from it. He felt a deep gratitude toward his younger brother, and he turned to wink at him.

"You're Okay Now, Bert."

"There he is!" Howard laughed, pointing across the stream. On the far bank, Ed was seated dejectedly on a log, staring out into the water. For a moment the two brothers tried to attract his attention, and then he looked up. A broad smile spread across his face, and he pointed upstream toward the dam.

"No," Bert yelled, shaking his head vigorously. "We'll go up there and shut off the water; then you can wade across." He saw Ed cupping his hand to his ear, as if he were having difficulty in hearing over the roar of the waters, and then he shook his head again. Ed, still smiling, and obviously relieved, nodded his assent and sat down again.

It was farther up to the end of the portage, where the canoe and duffle still rested high and dry, than Bert had realized. He stared in amazement at the tossing waters boiling down through the formerly placid pool where he had been fishing, and then started the uphill climb to the dam. Just as he reached the top of the spillway, a rickety Ford came rattling down a single-track road that came out of the woods and led to the back of the gatekeeper's cabin. Inside, at the wheel, was their acquaintance, and on his face was an angry scowl. He braked the car to a squealing stop, jumped out, and rushed over to Bert and Howard.

"Don't you know you could be put in jail for doing that?" he demanded in a shrill voice.

"Put in jail for doing what?" Bert asked blankly, his voice showing his surprise.

"For openin' them gates without permission, that's what for!" yelled the gatekeeper. "You've drawed down the level of the lake two feet more'n it's supposed to be!"

"Now wait a minute," interposed Bert, angry himself. "You think *we* opened the gates? Well, how do you suppose I got soaking wet? I'll tell you how—because *you* or somebody else up here opened the gates without warning us. If it hadn't been for my brother, I'd be floating downstream."

On the man's face, anger gave way to shock and amazement. He scratched his head and looked reflectively at the ground before staring at Bert again. This time, Bert noticed, he looked surprised. "Then you were downstream when the gates opened?" he asked incredulously.

"Sure," answered Bert. "We were fishing downstream. I was carried away, but my brother Howard saved me." He put his hand on Howard's shoulder as a token of appreciation.

"Well, let's go out and shut the gates, and then we'll talk about this some more." The gatekeeper walked lightly out on the stringers of the dam, put his hand to a giant wheel, and began to revolve it counterclockwise. With a grating sound, audible above the roar of the waters, the gate began to close slowly. As it closed, the sound grew less and less until, finally as the last of the flood disappeared around the bend, there was only the trickling of a tiny stream coming through cracks in the dam.

"That does it," muttered the keeper, "and since you didn't open that gate, I bet I know who did do it. At least, I've got a hunch."

"Who?" demanded Bert, smoothing back his fiery hair, and pushing one damp lock out of his eyes.

"Them two fellers that came through last night," the gatekeeper explained. "An old man and a youngster. They kept askin' me all about how the gate on the dam worked, and I even had to go out and show 'em which way the wheel turned. The old feller said he was a lumberman and wanted to put in a dam like this one."

"Great mackerel!" cried Bert excitedly. "You hear that, Howie? The Wallaces again!"

"The who?" asked the old gatekeeper. Bert quickly explained to him.

"By thunder!" shouted the keeper. "Those men are dangerous. And I know what to do about it, too." He turned on his heel and sprinted toward his house, ran lightly up the stairs and inside as the boys stared at each other. A moment later, they heard him crank the handle on the telephone and then his voice was raised in high-pitched but inaudible conversation. He came out, rubbing his hands.

"That'll fix 'em," he chuckled. "I phoned down to the ranger."

"What good will that do?" Bert asked, totally unimpressed. He stared at the keeper with a jaundiced eye.

"Good?" echoed the old man. "They're walkin' right into a trap. They don't know it, but there's a phone line down to the ranger cabin on Eagle Lake. When they come through there, he'll head 'em off and arrest 'em."

The news filled Bert with relief. "Thanks," he said to the keeper, and meant it. "Come on, Howie. Let's go down and meet Ed. Then we can go on with our trip."

Feeling better now, he ran down the path to the portage, with Howard following. He burst into the grassy little clearing, and then stopped short. Ed wasn't there!

"Something's wrong," he said, turning toward his younger brother. "The water's been down for fifteen minutes now. Surely Ed should have been able to get back upstream in that time, or he should have been able to cross where he was."

"That's right," Howard agreed. "It *is* funny. What d'you think we'd better do?"

"Let's just get in the canoe, without loading it, and paddle down a mile or two," Bert suggested. With Howard helping him, he lifted the canoe and dropped it in the water. He sat down in the stern, while Howard took the bow paddle, and they drifted easily out into the stream. The current was not fast, now that the dam had been closed; and, now and then, Bert guided the canoe toward shore and looked carefully for traces of Ed. He began to have a sinking feeling, and a conviction that something had gone wrong.

"I don't understand it," he finally said, leaning forward toward Howard as the canoe drifted down through a stretch of slack water. "He wouldn't deliberately go in the wrong direction. He knew we had gone upstream, and even if he couldn't hear what we said over the roar of the water, he could tell from the expression on my face." Howard grimly nodded assent, and then the two boys handled their paddles carefully as the canoe dropped down toward a small, rocky stretch. They shot through, between the boulders, at express-train speed. Ahead of them, the river curved to the left, and there was the roar of a larger rapids. On the left bank was an alder thicket and a little crescent of beach. Bert carefully guided the canoe in to a landing. As the bow grated, Howard leaped out and pulled it a little higher so Bert could disembark.

"Let's explore a little way on foot," Bert suggested. He swung around the corner, along the foaming rapids. The river here formed a smooth

but ominous-looking chute, which fed into a pool
overhung by ledges. The tan color of another bit of
sandy shore was visible below. As Bert peered downstream, shading his eyes, he thought that he saw a
movement. It almost looked as if someone were lying there on the beach, asleep.

"Ed," he said to himself, and burst through the
trees. Back there, away from the river, the forest was
dense, and the walking was not good. He passed swiftly behind the ledge and then forced his way through
the alders to the beach. His eyes hadn't deceived
him. Ed was asleep on a little sliver of beach, and his
clothes, too, were wet. He was not only asleep, but
he was snoring noisily, something he did only when
he was very tired. Bert almost hated to wake him,
but curiosity was more important than considera-
tion, and he gently bent down and shook his older
brother by the shoulder.

"Eh? What?" Ed murmured drowsily, and then
came awake with a start. He sat up so quickly that
he and Bert almost bumped heads. Bert, fortunately
for both of them, recoiled just in time.

"Don't tell me you're getting as careless as you
say I generally am," Bert chided him. "Or don't you
know the difference between downstream and upstream?"

"Why, sure I know the difference," Ed said calmly. "It just so happened that I was kidnaped."

"By whom?" Bert demanded.

His brother chuckled grimly. "Need you ask?"

"Tell me about it!" Bert sat down on the sand. Howard, who had followed him, stood silently watching them both.

"I was waiting for you to come back," Ed began, "when somebody grabbed me from behind and held my arms so I couldn't move them. I twisted my head around, and it was old Mr. Wallace, with Alan beside him.

" 'We're going to take you along with us,' he said to me, and he laughed. It was an awful-sounding laugh, Bert, believe me. Then he pushed me around so that I stood between him and Alan, and we started down along the stream. He didn't say much, and I was too frightened to ask any questions, but from one or two things he let drop to Alan, I figured the two of 'em had their canoe parked a little way downstream.

"Once or twice, we stopped and they began to ask me where you and Howie had gone. I wouldn't tell 'em a thing, and old man Wallace got pretty mad. His face got all red, and I thought he was going to hit me, but Alan calmed him down. He said they could use me as a decoy; that they could catch you and Howie separately.

"Well, we were going along above the ledge you just passed, and we came to a spot where we were really close to the river. I could see that there was deep water below, so I simply jumped sidewise and lit in the stream. I dived down, and came up on a little shelf under the ledge. I could hear them searching around, up above, but apparently neither one of them can swim. So, finally they went away, and I got mighty chilly and came out for a rest. That's how I happen to be here."

"I guess we'll have to be awfully careful from now on." Bert sighed. "At least, until we get to Eagle Lake. The ranger there is going to arrest Alan and his dad when they come through."

"And none too soon," said Howard. "Maybe we'd better wait a day or two until they've had time to get that far."

"Wait! Don't be silly!" Bert cried. "Let's be down there to see what happens. I don't think the Wallaces will try to take on all three of us. Come on, let's get the canoe back to the portage and load our stuff." He gestured widely with his right hand, and led the way over the top of the ledge to the beach where the canoe was grounded. Using their paddles to pull the canoe up through the little rapids, the boys reached their supplies half an hour later.

"Let's hurry!" shouted Bert. "We don't want to miss the show at Eagle Lake!"

CHAPTER TEN

THROUGH THE RAPIDS

Overhead the feathery branches of the pine trees arched out to filter the rays of the brilliant sun. The river had narrowed and flowed quietly between its banks, with just enough current so that Bert needed only to dip his paddle occasionally. In the half-shade, the water seemed to be black. With each stroke of the paddle, it parted, and then flowed back again almost silently. It was almost like being in church, Bert thought to himself, and he caught himself holding his breath, as if he expected somehow to hear the sound of organ music and the voices of the choir.

As the canoe swung around a curve in the stream, there was a splash, a snort, and then Bert was looking into the eyes of a moose, disturbed at his feeding. A little clump of weeds still hung from one corner of the animal's mouth. The current had quickened, and the boys shot by him, but Bert turned to stare. Annoyed at the invasion of his privacy, the moose was splashing sullenly ashore. The trees parted to receive him, but he could be heard crashing back through the underbrush.

"What a sight!" Bert gasped. "I never even

dreamed of seeing moose up here."

"Neither did I," remarked Ed, "but I did read that they're becoming more plentiful in Maine. They've had a closed season up here for many years, and I guess they're coming back again."

"D'you think he would have charged us if we'd stopped right there?" Bert asked.

"Well, they tell me that moose are generally more scared of you than you are of them," said his older brother. "But I have heard of an occasional moose going after a man. In that case, the best thing to do is to climb a tree—fast."

As Bert dipped his paddle again, he heard ahead of him a rumbling sound. "Must be another rapids," he announced. "Wonder which one it is?"

He looked back to see Ed extracting a much-folded map from his shirt pocket. As the canoe drifted slowly downstream, Ed studied the map intently.

"This is a tough one," Ed commented grimly, looking up from the map. "It's called Dead Man's Rapids, and I guess we'll have to portage."

Bert groaned. "Ouch! I still haven't gotten used to that tumpline. How long a portage is it?"

"About half a mile," answered his brother, and shook his head in commiseration. The noise of the rapids was growing louder, and as they rounded another bend, Bert could see how the river was narrowing down to a canyon. A spray hung over the canyon, and the sound of the tumbling water was multiplied a hundredfold. On the near bank there was a tiny clearing, with the blackened remains of a campfire. Obviously, Bert thought, this was the portage. Their canoe slid in to shore and, as it grated on the pebbles, Howard awoke from his doze in the middle of the canoe.

"Don't tell me it's another portage!" he moaned. "Wouldn't it be easier to walk down the river than to tote all this equipment?" He yawned, stretched his arms, and then helped steady the canoe alongside the bank while Bert and Ed climbed out and began to unload the duffle. Soon, all the equipment was piled on the shore, and Howard himself climbed out. He crouched down and held the canoe while Bert and Ed loaded packs on their shoulders.

"I'll bring the canoe down," he called to Bert, who was groaning under the weight of his load.

"Okay," said Bert, and started plodding down the long portage. The sandy path soon gave way to marsh, and every time Bert put his foot down it sank deep into the swale. The black flies were swarming furiously, and beads of perspiration stood out on Bert's forehead. *It's getting warmer,* he thought to himself, and glanced at the sky. A faint haze was creeping across the sun, the forerunner of a thunderstorm. Behind him, as he moved slowly along, he could hear Ed breathing deeply. At one point, as Bert balanced himself on a slippery log, he heard a splash and a grunt. He looked back to see Ed, flat in the swamp but still chuckling at his own clumsiness.

"Can I help you?" he called back.

"No, thanks," Ed's voice floated back to him. "I'll get up all right."

Bert waited until his older brother had climbed to his feet once more, and then resumed his plodding walk. He had forgotten to put more insect repellent on his neck, and he could feel the stinging sensation, as if a red-hot needle had suddenly been jabbed into him, as the swarming flies descended on him. Then the swamp gave way to an airy grove of Norway pine, whose straight trunks ascended toward the sky, and at the end of the grove he could see the river again. He gratefully dropped his load when he reached the riverbank, and sank down on the aromatic pine needles for a moment's rest.

"Hey!" came a frantic scream from somewhere back on the portage trail. It was loud enough to be audible over the roar of the rapids, and Bert felt a chill of apprehension. That was Howie! What could the trouble be? As he got to his feet, Howard came sprinting toward him.

"The canoe!" he gasped. "It got away from me, and it's in the rapids now!"

Bert ran to the riverbank and stared upstream.

His heart sank at what he saw. The river roared and
plunged through fang-like rocks. A man could not
live in that white fury of water. Could a canoe, even
one of metal, made with the utmost care, survive?
As he looked into the rapids, his question was answered. There was a silvery flash, and the canoe
came bouncing down through the rocks. By a mir-
acle, it twice escaped piling up on the sharp rocks,
and then floated free in the more quiet water below
the rapids.

"I'll have to swim for it," Bert called, and stripped
off his shirt. He quickly unlaced his shoes, and dived
into the icy water. Aerated in the rapids, the water
was so cold that he could feel a numb sensation
creeping up his arms. Then, gasping, he touched
the familiar metal of the canoe and laboriously began to swim toward shore with it. As his feet touched
bottom, Howard waded out and helped him to pull
it ashore.

"Well, I guess this is the end of our trip," Bert
declared bitterly, and then jumped with surprise as
he looked at the canoe. Filled with water though it
was, not a sign of a leak was evident. Quickly, with
Ed and Howard helping him, he turned the canoe
upside down and let the water drain out. Then, with
practiced fingers, they felt along the metal skin of
the canoe. Not a rivet had started, not a hole had
been torn.

"We certainly must be traveling under a lucky star." Bert sighed. "There are a couple of dents, and that's all." He turned and stared reprovingly at Howard. "How in the world did it happen, Howie?"

"Well, golly," stuttered Howard, digging his toe into the pine needles, "I was getting ready to pull the canoe up on shore when I saw a movement in the underbrush. I thought for a minute it might be the Wallaces, and I was so surprised I let go of the canoe. A second later a partridge flew up. I looked back for the canoe, but by that time she was already in the rapids."

"It'll teach you a lesson, anyway," advised Ed, who had been listening to this explanation with an amused quirk to his lips. "Never let go of a canoe. If that had been a canvas canoe, instead of one made of metal, we'd have had to hike back twenty miles through the brush."

"I'll never do it again," promised Howard earnestly.

"Be sure of that," added Ed, a little more sternly. "That canoe is the only link we have with civilization. Either way, back to the dam or down to the ranger's cabin on Eagle Lake, it's a mighty long hike, and we might never get out of the woods." He looked at his watch. "Gee whiz, it's two o'clock already. We certainly can't make it to Eagle Lake today."

Bert glanced at his own watch, and then looked around him more carefully. "Well," he suggested, "what's wrong with this for a campsite?"

"Okay with me." Ed checked their surroundings. "After we're settled here, how about a little fishing for the rest of the day."

"You've made a deal!" Bert and Howard agreed with a shout.

CHAPTER ELEVEN

A DARK-HAIRED STRANGER

When the boys rolled out of their sleeping bags in the morning, they were surprised and pleased to discover that their old friend Jed, the guide, had pitched his tent near theirs during the night.

Jed was busy at the campfire when the three boys besieged him with questions. "What are you doing up here, Jed? We didn't even hear you come in last night!"

"Well, I recognized your canoe and things and I thought you wouldn't mind if we joined you, so—"

"You said 'we,'" Bert interrupted the guide. "Who's with you, anyway?" As he spoke, a tousled head poked out of the doorway of the tent, and a dark-haired fellow in his late teens crawled out. He came forward with his hand extended.

"I'm Bob Grady," he greeted them, "and Jed is taking me down on a trip. Certainly glad to know you."

"I'm Bert Walton and these are my brothers, Ed and Howard." After the introductions Bert told Jed and Grady of their trouble at the dam.

"Those people wouldn't be unhappy if something

did happen to us," he added, dropping down to perch on a fallen pine log and looking up at Grady. "They tried to get rid of us out in Utah last spring, and didn't succeed, so now I guess they're trying to dispose of us out here in the woods. Their name is Wallace—Tom and Alan Wallace."

"Wallace!" gasped Grady, almost jumping in his surprise. "Why, I knew—" he stopped short, obviously confused, and turned to walk back toward the tent. Bert leaped up and started to walk alongside him.

"You know the Wallaces?" he asked. Evidently reluctant to answer, Grady bent his head to crawl into the tent, and dropped on all fours to go through the doorway.

"Yeah," his voice came back, oddly muffled by the folds of the tent, "I knew Alan. We went to school together down in Boston."

"Well, gee, tell me more about it!" urged Bert, sticking his head in the doorway. Grady had dropped down on a sleeping pad. As Bert looked at him, he returned Bert's stare, and then rolled over on his stomach, resting his head on his arm.

"I'd rather not talk about it," he said faintly. "I want to take a nap."

Bert felt a quickening twinge of suspicion. Grady burrowed his head deeper into the cushion of his arm, and obviously was determined not to answer.

"You Know the Wallaces?"

Bert backed out of the tent and composed his face as he stood up to stroll toward Jed and his brothers.

"Let's eat!" Howard yelled to him, and began to rummage in one of the duffle bags. Bert suddenly realized what he had forgotten for a moment—that he was hungry!

"And not a single fish to eat!" he mourned as he returned to his perch on the fallen log. Jed looked quickly at him and grinned.

"Well, I figgered you'd be hungry when you woke up," he said, reaching down into a pile of ferns beside the fire, "so this morning I went fishin'." He held up a freshly caught trout, already cleaned, its speckles glittering in the sunlight.

"Wow!" Bert exclaimed. "I can hardly wait!" Jed deftly split the trout and laid it out on a small broiling rack. Bert was ravenous with hunger, but he still could appreciate the beauty of the delicate pink flesh. As he watched, Jed laid a strip of bacon on each side of the fish, closed the broiling rack, and stood it against the fire. From a flat rock at the side of the flames, he lifted a pot and set it in the embers. In a moment, the blended aroma of heating cocoa and broiling fish drifted to Bert's nostrils.

"Have a plate," Jed urged him, holding out a slab of birch bark. The trout, by now, was sizzling briskly, and the bacon was soaking its fat into the flesh of the fish. Jed inspected the broiler with a practiced eye, lifted it off the fire and flipped it open. With a knife, he carefully split the fish into three equal portions and served it to the boys.

"I never in my life tasted anything so good!" said Bert. He licked his fingers to get the last, lingering taste of the fish, and with a sigh of gratitude reached forward to take from Jed's hands a steaming mug of cocoa. As he sipped it, the warmth seemed to permeate down through his whole body.

Jed, meanwhile, had pulled out his stumpy pipe and was puffing contentedly on it. Bert slipped down so that his back was resting against a log, and stole a look at his watch. It was only nine o'clock, though it seemed much later. He looked up to notice that Jed was watching him.

"What're your plans now?" Jed inquired. Bert lowered his voice.

"I don't want Grady to hear," he said. "I'm not sure that I trust him. But we want to get on to Eagle Lake to see if the Wallaces have come through there."

"I don't understand what you mean about Grady," Jed said in an equally low-pitched voice. "Even if he does know Tom Wallace, I still think he's a fine boy, and I'm sure he's got nothing to do with what's going on."

"Well, maybe so," admitted Bert, "but I'm suspicious of him. What do you think we ought to do,

Jed?" From the corner of his eye, he noticed that Bert and Howard were crowding closer, listening for the guide's answer. Jed puffed thoughtfully on his pipe, and sent up a cloud of tobacco smoke.

"Boys, if I were you, I'd take my time," he said finally. "My guess is that the Wallaces aren't too far away right now. There's a whole network of lakes and rivers in this country, and plenty of spots for 'em to hide out. You go direct to Eagle Lake, and you may frighten 'em away. My advice to you is to go along, have fun, and I'll keep an eye on you. I may not always be right behind you, but I'll be close by; and if you don't take any foolish chances, nothing will happen to you."

"Well, okay then," Bert said, feeling a little foolish about his suspicions of Bob Grady. "And I'm sorry I was so doubtful of Bob. If you say he's a good fellow, then he must be all right. I'm going in and say good-by to him." He rose to his feet and strolled over to the tent.

"Bob!" he called. There was a muffled grunt inside, and Bert crawled through the doorway. Bob was just as Bert had left him, his head pillowed on his right arm. Squatting on his haunches, Bert said rapidly, "Bob, I'm sorry. For a moment I thought you might have had some connection with the Wallaces. Now I've discovered that you don't, and I've come to apologize." He stuck out his hand, but Bob did not move.

"Oh, go away and don't bother me!" came his muffled voice. Astounded, Bert sat for a moment staring at the back of Grady's head, at his tousled, black hair, and his checkered shirt. Struck speechless, he finally withdrew his hand, swung around, and crawled through the doorway again.

"Now I'm more puzzled than I ever was," he said to himself as he composed his face, stood up, and walked back to the little cluster around the fire.

CHAPTER TWELVE

MOOSE BACK

No one looked up as Bert returned to the fire, and he discovered the reason quickly. Jed and his brothers were busy watching the strange antics of two grayish-blue birds with big beaks and a clumsy manner. Quite uninterested in the fact that humans were around, these two birds were busily engaged in picking up scraps of bread and bits of bacon, with which they flew to a near-by tree.

"Canada jays," said Jed quietly. "Some people call 'em camp robbers. They'll steal anything they can carry, anything that isn't nailed down. Look here."

From his pocket he pulled a shiny new penny, which glittered in the morning sun. He dropped it on the ground a few inches away from his feet. Immediately one of the birds swooped down, deftly picked it up, and flapped away to drop it in a nest in the crotch of an old pine tree.

"Guess we'd better stake down our canoe at the next stop," Bert said with a grin. "It's shiny enough for these birds to carry it away."

"Maybe so," agreed Ed, looking quizzically at

him. "But first let's get under way. It's after ten o'clock now, and we've still got a good distance to go before we reach Eagle Lake."

"You won't make it today, boys," Jed said. He rose to his feet and, from that dominant position, looked down on Bert, Howard, and Ed.

"Gosh, that's too bad!" said Bert, and there was genuine disappointment in his voice. "I'll bet the Wallaces are there by now."

"And I'll bet they aren't," insisted Jed. "I think they're hanging around some of these back ponds. What you'd better do is to take your time, and take it easy. I'll always be near by to keep an eye on you."

"What's below us, Jed?" asked Bert. A light breeze had sprung up, and it ruffled through his hair. He looked intently downstream where a faint mist, yesterday's rainstorm evaporating in the bland sunshine, overhung the water.

"Well," said the guide, scratching his grizzled chin, "you'll go down through a couple of small rapids, then through some still water for a few miles, and finally you'll come to the Penobscot Riff. That's a long rapids, where another river comes in. You can get through all right if you're careful. Tell you what—I'll follow along behind you. If you'll stop at the upper end of the Riff, I'll walk down alongside and show you how to get through." He stopped a minute and reflected.

"Say," he finally remarked to Bert, "have you fellows got a settin' pole? You could use it on these upper rapids where it's kind of shallow."

"What's a settin' pole?" asked Bert, his curiosity aroused. He rose to his feet and looked up at Jed, whose eyes already were glancing around the clearing, as if in search of something.

"I'll show you," Jed said, as he picked up an ax and walked across to a tall young maple about six inches in diameter. A few strokes and the sapling tumbled at his feet. Deftly, and with no effort at all, he clipped off the branches and chopped the narrower top loose. The result was a pole about ten feet tall, which he picked up and hefted reflectively in his hands.

"This is it," he demonstrated. "In the shallow water, where there's rocks, one feller stands in the front of the canoe and uses this settin' pole to control the boat. Comin' upstream, it's handy, too; it'll save you a lot of portages. Most of us guides will take one of these poles and put a steel tip on the end; that keeps the pole in shape longer. You'll have plenty of time to cut another one, though, when this one wears out."

He tossed the pole to Bert, who caught it with both hands and examined it closely, before turning to thank Jed. The guide acknowledged his thanks with a nod of the head and then walked back toward

the tent where Grady still lay sleeping, or, as Bert
concluded, where he probably lay listening to the
conversation. He still didn't trust their new-found
acquaintance, but he decided not to confide his suspicions further to his brothers.

By this time the canoe was resting in the water,
and Ed was carrying down the last load of duffle.
From a branch overhanging the bank, two Canada
jays watched them curiously. Bert couldn't help
grinning at their air of clumsy alertness. He carefully handed the setting pole to Howard, who was
already in position in the canoe, then held the craft
while Ed got in. He couldn't help admiring the deft-
ness with which Ed climbed into the stern, scarcely
disturbing the balance of the canoe. He climbed in,
himself, and the bow settled down under his weight.

"So long, Jed!" he called, and a muffled reply
came back from inside the tent. He picked up his
paddle and dipped it into the water, pulling it back
toward him. They were off again, on what strange,
new adventure Bert did not know. It always gave
him an odd sensation to be starting a new day's
travel in these woods; even if nothing exciting happened, it was still adventurous to be paddling down
a new stretch of river.

Ahead of them, sparkling in the sun, the river
rippled down around a bend, and then became calm
once more. Midway down this long reach of clear

water, faintly stained with the tan of the hemlock and spruce through which it flowed, a tiny stream tinkled down over the bank. Out a little way in the water was a sun-bleached log.

"Ought to be trout in there," Bert called back to Ed, who lifted his paddle from the water and let the canoe float idly. Ed's answer was to pull out his rod case and a little box of transparent plastic, through whose sides Bert could see a coil of leaders and a splash of color. These came forward to Bert, passed to him by Howard, who watched the proceedings with interest. Deftly, Bert joined his rod together, attached the reel below the cork butt-handle, threaded the golden line through the rings, and tied on a leader. He hesitated for a moment as he poked through the tangled mass of flies.

"Which one?" he asked. Ed's answer floated back to him on the calm morning air.

"Try a Mickey Finn," he suggested. "That's the yellow and red streamer."

Bert quickly picked out the Mickey Finn and attached it to the leader. With his left hand, he pulled free a length of line; then, with his right hand, he deftly cast in behind the log. He let the fly float on the water for a moment before beginning to retrieve it. There was a swirl, and then an immense head poked itself out of the water; the huge mouth of a trout seemed to close around the streamer. With a twitch of his right hand, Bert deftly tightened the line. Then, with a twinge of disappointment, he realized that the trout had not hooked himself.

"Missed!" he said gloomily. He looked back at Howard, who shook his head in commiseration. Ed, leaning back against the metal of the canoe, watched him calmly.

"Let the streamer float a little longer before you try to retrieve it," his older brother suggested. "That's a big fellow, but he's not very hungry. He just 'lipped' the fly. Maybe if you let him roll it around in his mouth a second longer, and then set your hook, things will be different."

Bert pulled in the free line with his left hand, and then cast again. This time the streamer hesitated for a moment on the smooth top of the log before dropping into the dark water on the other side. Again, Bert could detect a movement in the little pool. Again, the huge head appeared; again, the huge mouth folded over the streamer. Restraining an impulse to yank at the line, he sat quietly for a second and then, very deliberately, tightened the line.

"Got him!" he yelled in his excitement as he felt the weight of the fish on the free line in his left hand. Slowly, he let the line run out, and then his rod bent under the pressure of the frightened trout, battling for freedom.

"Keep your tip high and don't let him get the

line wound around the log!" came Ed's judicial, always calm, voice from the back of the canoe. Automatically, Bert lifted the rod and released a little more line with his left hand. The rod almost doubled on itself, but as the fish turned and lunged, seeking to free itself from this strange captor, Bert kept the line taut; now and then releasing a little, now and then tightening the line. Gradually, very gradually, he could feel the fish tiring. Its runs shortened, its pressure against the line lessened. He was able, bit by bit, to reel in a little.

"I think he's just about ready to be hauled in," he flung over his shoulder at Ed. "Why don't you paddle alongside the log and hand me the net?"

As he swiftly reeled in his line, the canoe drew up to the log, grating against it. On the other side, still deep in the water, Bert caught a flash of bronze and red, his trout, sulking in the shadows. His rod bent again as he wound at the reel, but this time there was no answering lunge on the sensitive line. He felt a pressure on his back; with his left hand, he reached around to grasp the landing net, which he dipped into the water. With his right hand, he lifted the rod high.

"It's a whale, not a trout!" he yelled as the exhausted fish came out into the sunlight. Quickly, he moved the net forward, and then lifted up on it until he felt the weight of the fish. It was almost too much for his one hand to lift.

"Here," he said to Howard, "hold the rod." Howard leaned forward and took the rod from his tired hand as he grasped the handle of the net. With a mighty heave, he lifted the net clear of the water and dropped the gasping fish into the bottom of the canoe.

"That's the biggest fish I've ever seen!" shouted Ed, roused from his usual calm. It was, indeed. The heaving sides of the trout, speckled brilliantly in reds and greens, shaded off into a scarlet belly. Its back was a golden bronze color. As Bert reached into the net to disengage the hook, Howard fumbled in his pocket and came out with a metal measure. Bert watched as his younger brother lengthened this measure to its full twenty-four inches and laid it alongside the trout. It did not quite reach.

"Good gravy!" exclaimed Bert, amazed at his own catch. "That fish must be twenty-six inches long!"

"Yeah, and it must weigh at least five pounds," said Ed, leaning forward to look at the speckled beauty. "Tonight, we'll skin it and pickle the skin in salt. When we get back to civilization, you can have the skin stuffed and mounted. Won't the boys down home be surprised to see a fish that size?"

"Yeah," said Bert, feeling a surge of pride. "Now I'll be satisfied if I never catch another fish." He unjointed the rod, removed the reel, and handed it back to Ed. He looked quickly at his wrist watch, and whistled shrilly. "Jeepers," he said, "it took me nearly an hour to get that fish into the boat. It's eleven-thirty now!"

"That's right," Ed concurred. "We'd better quit fishing and get down to the Riff. Jed can't be far behind us."

Around the corner, the river boiled down through a short rapids, where boulders showed on either side.

"It should be time to try out the settin' pole," remarked Bert. He reached back and picked up the pole, and then stood up in the bow, bracing himself by spreading his legs. He was surprised to see how much more clearly he could pick out the rocks.

"Okay," he said confidently to his brothers, "I'll take over." The canoe began to gather speed. Bert thrust the pole deep in the water, and felt it grate against the gravel at the bottom of the river. Ahead of him the river dropped swiftly through a narrow channel. As Bert swung the setting pole from one side of the canoe to the other, he felt more and more confidence in its use. Time and again, he just missed ramming the canoe into the rocks. Each time, the setting pole saved him from disaster. Finally the stream widened and flowed swiftly down through the last rocks into another quiet pool.

"That does it," Bert flung back to his brothers as

he lifted the setting pole from the water and sat down on the front seat of the canoe. In the back of the canoe, he could see Ed lifting his paddle, and he relaxed. As they drifted lazily down through the still water, he glanced back once more and pointed his right hand toward the rapids they had just come through. Behind them, Jed and Grady were making the same run. Bert could not help admiring the sureness and skill with which Jed used his pole. He waited expectantly as the other canoe shot out into the quiet water and drew alongside them.

"We'll sort of paddle alongside a while," Jed said. "Maybe we'll see some more moose down through here. Usually they feed on the water plants just around the bend."

The two canoes floated together. Grady kept his face turned away from Bert, as if avoiding him, but Jed chatted cheerily. As they rounded a bend, the guide put his finger to his lips. Just ahead, two moose were feeding, their heads deep in the water. Even though the canoes drifted quietly, one of the huge animals looked up and snorted. It was a mammoth bull moose with a spreading rack of antlers. Instead of turning to head for the shore, he started wading into deeper water. At this point, the stream widened into a small pond.

"Watch this!" said Jed, and his canoe shot ahead with powerful strokes until he came alongside the swimming moose. As Bert and his brothers watched, popeyed, Jed leaped from the canoe and grasped the antlers. He deftly swung one leg over the moose's back, held onto the antlers with one hand; and, with the other, lifted his battered hat from his head and emitted a whoop, like a cowboy riding a bucking bronco.

"Just look at that!" cried Bert, transfixed with admiration. The frightened moose kept swimming toward the farther shore, and Jed continued to let out his ear-splitting whoops. Just as the moose began to rise out of the water, Jed slipped from his back and dropped into the water with a splash. He rose, grinning, and beckoned the two canoes to join him. The broad back of the amazed moose was just disappearing into the underbrush as the two canoes grated on the shore.

"That's the best show I've ever seen!" Bert cried happily. "Better than any wild west movie!"

Jed, dripping and beaming, shook himself like a water-soaked dog and a fine shower of spray fell from his clothes. "Makes me feel young, too," he contributed. "I haven't tried riding a moose in twenty years. Probably won't ever get another chance."

As Bert stared at him, admiration in his eyes, a rifle cracked, far off in the stunted tree. The look of pleasure on Jed's face vanished, and an angry frown

"Watch This!" Jed Whooped

replaced it.

"Somebody huntin' out of season!" he said stern-ly. "Nobody but a poacher would do a thing like that! Certainly nobody who lived in Maine."

A thought flashed into Bert's mind, and his lips silently formed the words, *Wallace!* He looked intently at Jed, and the old guide's right eyelid dropped, ever so slowly, as if to acknowledge Bert's unspoken suspicion. Bert glanced quickly back at Grady. The dark-haired boy was looking sullenly upstream.

Wonder how much he knows? Bert asked himself silently. More than ever, he wanted to accuse Grady directly. He was about to speak when he glanced back at Jed. The old guide looked straight at him, his blue eyes seeming to look through Bert, and he slowly shook his head. Bert flicked his glance at Grady, who still stared upstream, and then looked back as Jed put his finger to his lips.

CHAPTER THIRTEEN

AN UNEXPECTED LOG RUN

The sun still shone brightly as Bert and his brothers pulled away from the shore of the pondlike spot where Jed had ridden the moose. Howard, awakened from his drowsiness, was chattering gaily. He lifted the trout high in the air so Jed could see it, and almost overbalanced the canoe in his restlessness.

"Take it easy, bub," Bert finally said to him. "We've still got a long way to go, and I'd hate to swim it." Howard subsided, but his eyes were still sparkling with animation, and Bert noticed that his younger brother's snub nose was twitching as it always did when he was restless.

The canoe shot down through swift water, following the path laid down by Jed, who was rhythmically paddling just ahead of them. A broad wake of bubbles spread out behind Jed's canoe, like a magic carpet on which Bert and his brothers were following. The forward canoe headed for the shore at a sun-baked little clearing, and Jed, with one final stroke, shot it up on shore as Bert and Ed followed suit.

"Time for lunch," Jed said to Bert. "How about

eating some of that trout?"

"Suits me," Bert said. "But I want to save the skin."

"That's all right," said Jed, leaning forward to pick up the trout. He carried it up the bank, pulled his hunting knife from its sheath, and carefully skinned the fish, laying the pink flesh on a strip of birch bark. Quickly, he started a fire, dug a frying pan from his capacious pack, and dropped a little butter into it. In a moment the trout was sizzling and sputtering.

"Come an' get it!" called Jed, and the hungry boys needed no urging. From their own packs they dug their plates, their knives, forks, spoons, and cups. Each took a generous helping of fish. Jed, meanwhile, had mixed up a creamy, yellow batter which he poured into a tin pie dish and set to bake in a reflector oven. The fierce heat of the fire worked quickly, and in a few minutes each boy handed forward his plate for a portion of johnnycake.

"Have some maple syrup," said Jed, offering an opened can. Each boy poured a generous quantity of syrup over the fluffy johnnycake and sat back to enjoy it. Bert sighed with satisfaction as he finished his portion. He leaned lazily against a fallen tree. As he shut his eyes and dozed, he could hear the cheerful clatter of dishes being washed. He dropped into a deeply pleasant slumber, from which he was awakened by the touch of a hand on his shoulder.

"Just thought I'd talk about the rest of the trip with you," Jed's voice came to him through the fog of awakening. "Just below here, the Robinson River comes in. They've been logging upstream, and there's a lot of pulpwood piled up above a dam a short distance. I don't trust that dam too much, and I think we ought to move down to Penobscot Riff as fast as we can."

"Are you going to show us how to get through the Riff?" Bert asked, pushing himself up to a sitting position as Jed crouched beside him, puffing on his pipe.

"I think you can just follow me down through," said Jed. "Keep about five hundred feet behind me, and you'll be all right."

"Okay," said Bert, glancing at his wrist watch. "It's one o'clock now, so I suppose we ought to get started pretty soon." He got to his feet, and looked around for his brothers. They were standing beside the fire, looking down into the crackling flames. Grady was off at a corner of the clearing, staring out into space. *Unsociable guy,* Bert thought to himself with a twinge of irritation.

"Okay, let's go!" he called to his brothers. Howard picked up a pack and started for the canoe, but Jed's voice halted him.

"Hold on a second," said the guide. "Let's put

the fire out first. You never want to leave a fire burning, boys. Always wet it down good, and then scatter it." He handed a pail to Howard, who sprinted for the water's edge and came back more slowly with a brimming pailful of water. Jed poured it on the fire. A cloud of steam arose, and he kicked the blackened logs apart with his moccasined feet.

"That does it," he grunted finally. "Now, let's go, Grady."

"Remember," was Jed's parting word as he pulled away from the shore, "keep going fast until you hit the Riff, and then follow me." Bert nodded and got into his own canoe.

Around the bend, a turbid stream came in from the right, its waters dark with the brown muskeg swamps and the far forests. That was the Robinson River. Bert stared upstream, looking for the dam. In the distance, he caught a glimpse of rapids through which the black water mumbled uneasily, and the grayish timbers of a dam. A second later they had shot past the river's mouth; but, in that second, Bert's heart leaped. He was certain he had seen someone atop the dam, staring downstream.

"I'm getting the Wallace family on my brain," he said impatiently to himself, and applied himself anew to his paddling. The water through which they were moving was still, and flowed with long, licking currents. But what was that faint, rumbling sound? Could they be so close to Penobscot Riff? It didn't make sense, for the map had told Bert that the big rapids was several miles downstream. The rumbling sound grew louder.

"Bert! Bert, look!" came Ed's voice, cracking with panic. Bert swiveled his head to look back. Down into the steady current, a wall of logs was pouring. Someone had opened the Robinson River dam, and they were trapped! For a blank moment Bert's mind refused to function, and then in the instant of danger he thought more clearly and coldly than ever before.

"Pull for the shore!" he commanded, and let out a yell. "Jed! In back of you!" He caught a glimpse of Jed's tanned face, and even in the distance separating them, it seemed to him that the guide's countenance whitened, and his steady paddle strokes faltered. As Bert bent to his paddle, so did Jed, and the two canoes shot toward the shore. Behind them, the rumble grew louder. Bert paddled furiously. The shore was only a few lengths ahead. Behind him, there was a booming sound, and then a fierce jolt. As he swung his head, he saw Ed topple into the water, and then the canoe grated on shore. He leaped out onto the sand, almost automatically, and yanked the canoe three feet up from the edge of the water as the first group of tawny-colored logs grated along the sand before bouncing out into the main current again. Out in the welter of logs, he could see Ed's blond head, bobbing on the turbulent current, and then it disappeared from sight.

Just below him, there was a jagged mass of rock sticking out of the water.

"Let him reach that rock!" Bert prayed. "Just let him reach that rock!"

As he stared out into the water, his heart jumped with elation. Ed was dragging himself painfully up onto the rock. Sodden as a drenched rat, the oldest of the Walton brothers clambered up to the top, and hung there just as the main tide of logs crashed against the rock with a grinding sound.

"He's safe!" Bert yelled over the thunder of the logs. "He's safe!" He embraced Howard and thumped him on the back. Downstream a little distance, Jed caught his eye and waved cheerily to him. He and Grady also were safe. As Bert started down the shore on a dead run, he glanced out again at Ed. His older brother had even saved the paddle. He was waving with it to those ashore.

Jed's face was split with a wide grin as Bert came up to him. He stuck out a calloused hand.

"Mighty nice thinking," he said. "If you hadn't hit for shore when you did, we'd all be gone. Soon's this log run passes, Ed can swim back to shore again. Guess we'd better camp here for the night, though, and let all the logs go through. I told you I didn't trust that dam, and I was right. Funny she gave way just at that moment, though."

"It's not funny at all," Bert blurted out. "I think that—" He caught Grady's eye and noticed that the dark-haired boy was leaning forward, his ears pricked up, with more attentiveness than Bert ever before had seen him register. Abruptly he stopped.

"Let's get some firewood, Jed," he suggested to the guide, and, grasping Jed by the arm, walked back into the woods a few paces with him. When he was sure that Grady was out of hearing distance, he blurted out his suspicion that the Wallaces had opened the dam. Jed's face darkened with wrath, and he clenched his hamlike hands.

"If I ever catch up with those two fellers—" he raged, and then calmed himself. He unclenched one hand, and laid it reassuringly on Bert's shoulder.

"Don't worry, son," he said. "Give 'em enough rope, and they'll hang themselves. That kind of feller always does. We'll just go ahead as if nothing had happened."

Out in midstream, as Bert and Jed approached the shore line again, the logs were thinning out. A little distance upriver, Bert could see open water, broken only by an occasional piece of pulpwood that bobbed lazily in the stream. Along the shore line, the water had gone down; and, on the rock, Ed was sitting with his eyes fixed attentively on his brother.

"Come on in!" yelled Bert. Ed slid down off the rock, paddle in hand, and began to swim. He came out beside them on a sandy spit, drenched but smiling. As he got to his feet, he dropped the paddle and flung his arms around his brother.

"Boy, I thought I was a goner for a little while!" he said, with a heartfelt note in his voice. He ran a hand over his bedraggled hair, and then, taking off his checkered shirt, began to wring it out.

"How's the paddle?" asked Bert, picking it up and hefting it in his hands.

"It's all right," said his older brother. "I was worried, too, so I checked it over carefully. But how's the canoe?"

"Golly, I never even thought about that!" said Bert, dropping to his knees beside the gleaming canoe. He ran his hand over a dent at the stern.

"Must have been a glancing blow," he finally said, looking up at Ed. "There's a big dent, which won't do any harm, but none of the rivets have been started. Our packs are wet, but we didn't lose any of them."

"Talk about luck," said Ed fervently. "We've had nothing but luck since we started this trip."

"That's right, boys," Jed said solemnly. "And now, let's get camp set up for the night. We can't make it through the rapids before dark, so we'd better settle down here."

Dinner came early, because Jed said they all deserved it, and the main dish again was trout, but with mealy potatoes baked in the fire and hauled out to be drenched with butter. Again Grady ate silently and by himself. The rest of the party, by common consent, ignored him.

"Time to go to bed, boys," said Jed after dinner. He knocked the last ashes from his pipe, winked at Bert, and disappeared into his tent, followed by Grady. Bert reluctantly got to his feet, shook his two dozing brothers into wakefulness, and led the way to bed.

CHAPTER FOURTEEN

A SHATTERED PADDLE

As Bert awoke, he could hear the patter of drizzling rain. By twisting in his sleeping bag, he could look out through the door into a gray, dreary morning. The spruce and balsam stood mournfully around the clearing, and even their branches seemed to droop in the mist. Far off, there was the grumble of thunder. Bert shivered, and burrowed deeper into his sleeping bag; for a moment, he dropped off again into a doze, and then he was wide awake. He glanced at his watch. It was eight o'clock.

"Good gravy!" he blurted out, and crawled quickly out of the bag. The moist, clammy air pressed down suffocatingly on him. He hated wet days in the woods, meals eaten in the crowded shelter of a tent, paddling with a poncho that kept off the rain but still let a few drops trickle down the front of your neck. Yet they had to go on. He tiptoed over to waken Howard, whose mouth was wide open, and then shook Ed's shoulder.

"Aw, let's spend today in our sleeping bags," Howard said drowsily. "It's no fun paddling in the rain."

"Maybe not, but we ought to keep going," said Bert. "I don't like it around here. It's sort of spooky. I'd like to get downstream farther before some more logs let loose on us."

"What made the dam break just as we were going through?" Howard inquired curiously, his high-pitched voice carrying out into the mist. Bert glanced out the door, where he saw Grady moving around a smoky fire, and laid a finger on his lips.

"I'll tell you later," he said in a low voice. Howard's eyebrows shot up. He knew, Bert thought to himself. He realized that the Wallaces were to blame. Bert struggled into his clammy clothes, pulled a poncho over his head, and walked out into the rain. Grady grunted what might have been a "Good morning," and then applied himself to the stirring of a pot full of oatmeal. Bert rummaged for his eating utensils, and held out a plate into which Grady dropped several huge spoonfuls of oatmeal.

"Looks as if it might clear before the day's over," Jed said encouragingly, looking at Bert from beneath his bushy eyebrows. Bert managed to grin back at him. He moved closer to the fire and spread out his hands to absorb some of its warmth. Behind him, he could hear the clatter of dishes as Howard and Ed served themselves. Drops of water sputtered into the fire, but the sound of the rain seemed to be lessening; and, before breakfast had ended, there was only a fine mist, hanging over the clearing and shrouding the dripping trees. Underneath his poncho, Bert was perspiring, and he was eager to be off, but Jed persistently lingered until he had sent the last puff of smoke from his pipe swirling up into the enveloping branches. Finally, he leaned over, tapped the bowl of the pipe on his upturned boot heel, and stuffed the pipe in his pocket.

"I'll lead, Bert," he said. "You fellows just follow me. We'll stop just at the top of the Riff, and I'll point out the way through; then you can trail me down." He slouched down the hill to his canoe, gestured at Grady to get in the bow, and pushed off into deeper water. A minute later, Bert and his brothers also floated away from the shore. In the distance, the eastern sky was growing brighter, but a sharp roll of thunder and a brief, but torrential, downpour served to remind everyone that the storm had not yet finished.

"That must be the clearing-up shower," Howard said. The last of the rain was skittering across the water, and it was followed by a shaft of sunshine so bright that he involuntarily flung one arm over his eyes to shield them. Immediately, however, the clouds swept across the face of the sun again. Ahead of him, Jed and Grady paddled steadily, and Bert was hard put to keep up with them. They swept down through long, misty reaches of river, dropped down through two small rapids where the setting pole had to be used, and finally obeyed the signal of Jed's uplifted paddle to swerve in to shore. Downstream, the Penobscot Riff grumbled angrily; and once, when the sun popped out, the flying spray of the first section of rapids made a glittering rainbow above the sheer rock walls that hemmed in the torrent of water.

"Come up here with me," Jed said to Bert and Ed, leading the way up a slippery clay path. At its top, he pushed through the underbrush to the edge of the ledge, and pointed downstream. Bert drew in his breath with a gasp. Nothing, it seemed to him, could live in that boiling caldron of water. For a moment, absorbed with his fears, he almost forgot to listen to Jed.

"—down through the middle of the channel," the guide was saying, "and then swing sharp left around that big rock spur in the middle. Gets easier after that, and you can just follow me."

"Okay," said Bert, numbly, "but it still frightens me."

"Well, it's safe if you follow in my track," Jed said reassuringly, looking into Bert's eyes. "Just keep paddling, and watch out for rocks. Otherwise, it's a three-mile portage, and you'd just be wearing yourself out carrying your duffle all that distance."

Bert swung around and, followed by Ed and the

guide, slid and ran back to the canoes. Howard, sitting quietly in the middle of the boat, for once asked no questions, and Bert preferred not to talk to him, suspecting that the quaver in his voice might give him away.

"Let's go," said Jed, calmly seating himself in his canoe. He waited until Bert and Ed had resumed their positions in the bow and stern respectively before pushing out from shore. A moment later Bert felt the water tug at his own canoe and draw it into the rushing funnel of Penobscot Riff. His eyes glued on Jed's back, he paddled furiously. The canoe swept down, bobbing like a cork, through the first funnel, and Bert could almost feel his paddle bend with the effort as he put all his weight on it to avoid the immense finger of rock that struck terror to his heart as it rose from the middle of the stream. The canoe seemed a living thing, running under its own power. The black walls of the rock spur slid by them, and then they were diving down a foaming channel where the sides of the stream elbowed each other and seemed to overhang the water. Bert put all his energy into his paddling. Now and then the flying spray blinded his eyes, but he did not have time to wipe it away.

Over the roar of the rapids came a wild cry from Ed, in the stern, and then the canoe began to turn sideways. Bert looked back, only for a second. What

he saw chilled his blood. Ed was holding up the remains of his paddle. It had split lengthwise, and
they were helpless in the rapids. Just ahead, another
saw-toothed spur of rock split the stream, which
boiled and rumbled to either side. Instinctively,
Bert snatched the setting pole. He held it firmly out-
thrust, from his sitting position, and the shock of its
contact with the spur almost threw him from the
canoe, which lurched and reeled but remained upright.

I've got to do it, he thought to himself, clenching
his teeth. *I've got to do it. We'd never live if we
upset in this water.*

Another great spur of rock rose in his path, and
to one side the water rose in a great, boiling mass.
Bert shut his eyes and thrust out the setting pole.
The shock of its contact sent a shooting pain through
his right arm and shoulder, but he held on, and
opened his eyes to see the canoe bouncing half-side-
ways through the watery haystack and out into another funnel. Just to his right, the water poured
over a massive rock. To his left, Jed and Grady were
gliding, like an eel, down a swift but smooth channel. Again, he thrust out his setting pole; and, this
time, the canoe seemed to shudder and stop. The
force of the blow knocked the setting pole from his
hand, and it disappeared in a welter of foam.

Bert grasped wildly for his paddle. He took two

strokes, three strokes, and then the canoe turned sidewise. *It's the end,* he thought numbly. *It's the end.* He closed his eyes and waited. The last thing he saw was Ed's face, with his older brother's mouth set in a grim line, and the expression of panic and fear printed on Howard's freckled face. And then the canoe was rocking in still water. He opened his eyes, scarcely believing what he saw. The river had widened just enough to permit the canoe to go through sidewise, and then had contemptuously spat out these strangers who dared to challenge it. A tongue of current had whirled them sidewise into a pool of clear, cool, translucent water. As Bert stared around him, the sun came out again, and the clouds began to boil over the horizon. The storm was over, and they were safe. A little downstream, Jed and Grady were waiting.

"Hand me the paddle, Bert!" Ed's crisp words interrupted Bert's reverie. He passed back his own paddle, still intact, and the canoe began to move again, this time in still water, until it came abreast of Jed's own canoe.

"What happened?" Jed asked. "I could see you were in trouble, but there wasn't anything I could do about it."

Ed reached down and held up the shattered paddle. It had split lengthwise.

"Lucky thing I always carry an extra paddle

along," Jed said quietly. He reached down and pulled another paddle from its resting place along the thwarts. He handed it across to Bert, who said, "Gee, thanks!" and hefted it admiringly.

"Now, let's pull in to shore and take a little rest," said Jed. "I'm still curious about that broken paddle. Let's look at it there."

The two canoes slid in to shore, and Bert stepped out somewhat shakily, but not neglecting to pull the metal canoe up on the sand. There was a little patch of marsh grass, with sandy dunes sticking through occasionally, and he sat down on one of these to take off his poncho and relish the drying warmth of the sun. Jed, meanwhile, was inspecting the shattered paddle carefully.

"Just as I thought," he finally said. "Look here." Bert looked closely at the end of the paddle. There was a narrow cleft there that puzzled him, and he lifted his head to look inquiringly at Jed.

"A chisel did that," Jed said. "Someone wanted to start the grain just enough to make the paddle split. And they succeeded, I must say. If that paddle had busted a few minutes earlier, none of you would be sitting here to tell the tale."

Bert lifted his head and stared at Grady, who was standing down by the bank. He felt his blood pulse angrily into his cheeks, and his heart began to pound as it always did when he was enraged. Before anyone could stop him, he jumped to his feet and ran down to confront Grady.

"You—you did this!" he spluttered. "Things happened to us before you showed up, but never so often and never such terrible things. When I asked you about the Wallaces, you wouldn't talk. And now—now you try to kill us! What's the matter, Grady, why do you hate us so?"

A faint flush appeared on Grady's face, but still he did not speak.

"Answer me!" Bert fairly yelled. "Or are you afraid to answer because you know you're guilty?"

"No," Grady finally said in a low voice. "I'm not guilty. You've got to believe me, I'm not. If I don't talk to you about Alan Wallace, it's because I have a reason. You can believe that or not, just as you wish."

"I heard somebody moving around last night," Bert shouted. "Was it you, Grady? Were you talking to the Wallaces, or were you down there trying to split this paddle with a chisel?"

"No," muttered Grady. "I was in my tent, and I stayed there all night. I don't hate you fellows; you've got to believe that. But if you don't trust me, then Jed and I will have to go on ahead." As Bert watched him, he signaled to Jed, who came walking toward him.

"Jed," he said, "these boys don't trust me. I don't

"You—You Did This!"

know whether or not *you* trust me, but I hired you as my guide, and you're still working for me. Come on; let's go." As Bert watched, Jed looked across at him, shrugged his shoulders, expressively thrust out his hands, and began to tote the duffle down to the canoe.

"So long, Bert," he said quietly as he finished his last trip.

"So long," said Bert, feeling a lump in his throat. He watched morosely as Jed's canoe pulled away, and then walked back to rejoin his brothers.

"Maybe I was wrong," he said as he sat down on a log beside them. "Maybe Grady isn't to blame. But there's something funny going on. Now that Jed knows how I feel, no doubt he'll keep an eye on Grady."

"Well, we're all in this together," Howard said, and Bert felt the pressure of an arm flung around his shoulder. "If we have to, we'll take turns keeping watch at night. I don't feel very sleepy, anyway."

"We'll make out," Bert said decisively. "One thing about it: The Wallaces always try to make each of these things look like an accident. They're afraid to do anything to us directly. So let's keep our eyes peeled for accidents, and we'll get along all right until Eagle Lake. Once we hit there, our troubles are over."

"That's just another two days' travel," broke in

Ed, who was consulting his water-soaked map. "To-day let's paddle on down to Mud Pond Landing and hike in for some fishing."

"Yeah." Howard grinned.

CHAPTER FIFTEEN

THE ENEMY CAMP

Mud Pond Landing was easily recognized. A brackish little stream emptied into the main river just above a clearing where dead trees stood stark and isolated in a clearing of waving grass. Off at one side was a tumble-down cabin which, on inspection, proved to be inhabited by porcupines.

"Ugh," shuddered Bert. "Doesn't look very promising to me. I just hope things are a little better up at Mud Pond than they are here." On a tree stub, a crudely lettered sign with a wavy arrow pointed the way toward Mud Pond, and there was even the evidence of a path.

"Do we dare to leave our stuff here without a guard?" Bert mused. "Or should one of us stay behind?" He looked appraisingly at Ed and Howard, both of whom showed by their expressions that they wanted to go along. "I guess the Wallaces won't bother us in bright daylight. Let's all go." He moved across the clearing, sending up a cloud of flies. Behind him, Ed was withdrawing the two fly rods from their case, and assembling the reels, fly boxes, and other equipment—not overlooking a bottle of fly dope, which he held up and carefully inspected as Bert watched him.

Beyond the swamp near their camp was a tiny rise of ground. At its crest, Bert stopped and said, "Gosh! Look at this!"

His brothers came silently up to him, and all three of them stared out at the scene before them. A tiny lake, rimmed by sand, nestled under hills that were cloaked from base to summit in virgin white pine. The water of this pond was crystalline; out in the distance, there was a single ripple where a trout lazily rose, snapped at a fly, and sank back again. It was a perfect picture of wilderness solitude; as Bert looked around him, he began to realize what all this northern forest must have been like before fire, and the lumberman, replaced the virgin timber with second-growth trees.

"It almost seems a sacrilege to talk," Bert finally said, and he did speak in a low voice. As he moved toward the shore, where an ancient raft rested on the sand, he took from Ed's hands his rod, reel, and fishing tackle. On the raft, there even were two crude paddles. That made it perfect, Bert reflected. With the help of his brothers, he pushed the raft out into deeper water, and made sure that it floated.

"Not quite as elegant as our own canoe," he said with a grin, "but it'll transport us." They floated out into deeper water. Bert tied a Royal Coachman to his leader and cast idly toward a little island, the only one on the lake. Immediately the water swirled, and he had a fish. In this clear, cold water, the fish was scrappy, though not so large as Bert's record trout. In an hour, all three boys had gotten as many fish as they could possibly eat.

Later, back at their campsite, the three boys cleared a space and in a few minutes had a crackling fire under way. Broiled trout, fried potatoes, and a steaming pot full of cocoa took care of the hunger their trip to Mud Pond had generated. After eating, Bert loosened his belt, leaned back, and sighed luxuriously.

"It's still not too late to go on a little farther," he said consulting his wrist watch. "It's still early in the afternoon. Ed, is there another campsite a few miles downstream where we might settle down for the night?" He looked inquiringly at his older brother.

"Why, sure," Ed replied after studying his wrinkled map for a minute. "There's a campsite marked some four miles downstream, and there's even another little pond not far back from the river."

"Oh, boy!" yelled Bert. "Let's go, then. I'd like to cut the barb off a hook and fish for trout just to see how many I can catch."

"Gee, but what would we do with 'em?" broke in Howard, his face wrinkled in puzzlement. "They'd spoil before we could eat 'em."

"Don't be a dope, Howie," Bert answered. A grin lit up his face. "All I want to do is to catch 'em and then throw 'em back in again. As long as I use a barbless hook, they won't be hurt."

"Oh, well, in that case—" sighed Howard, and reluctantly got to his feet. "Let's go!" he called, and Bert and Ed rose and walked down to join him in the canoe. They paddled out into midstream, where the current took them, and began their trip once more. Almost imperceptibly, as they dropped down river, the timber on the banks began to change. Clumps of pine and spruce gave way to smaller second growth, and this in turn to tall, burned spars and finally to a mass of impenetrable brush.

"Look at that," said Bert, gesturing with a paddle. "A forest fire has been through here, and not too long ago. We'll have to watch sharp for the campsite. The map must have been made before the fire came through."

The river had deepened now and flowed more swiftly. On the left, a brook came tumbling down over a ledge, and, as Bert glanced at it, he heard Ed's voice, and turned to see his older brother consulting the map.

"The campsite should be about half a mile below us, on the right-hand side," Ed called out. "Another brook comes in there. Keep a sharp lookout so we don't run past it. The map shows swamps below us, for a long distance."

A few minutes later, a grassy swale opened out on the right, and a stream was visible, meandering down through it. Two tall saplings, stuck into the ground and crossed at the top, showed where some previous canoeing party had made camp. The prow of the canoe slid into unresisting mud; and, as Bert jumped out, he sank in almost over his boot tops.

"Ugh," he said disgustedly, "I hope the campsite will be drier than it is down here by the river." He scrambled up the bank, and noted with delight that the swale itself was dry, though even more infested by flies than the previous campsite.

"Let's get a smudge going," he suggested, reaching in his pocket for the bottle of fly dope, and dabbing it vigorously on his sun-reddened face. Without waiting to unload the canoe, Howard and Ed sprinted for the encircling trees to pull loose some green branches. In a few minutes, a spurt of flame shot up from their campfire, and then this was drowned out by a dense cloud of smoke. As Bert looked around him, seeking to locate himself, he noticed that the blackened remains of another campfire were near by. Quite involuntarily, he walked over and kicked at them with his boot. A thin trickle of smoke rose up, and he could see the dully glowing eye of one ember still winking at him.

Someone had camped here not long before, and a narrow pathway where the grass was bent over showed that they had walked on in toward the pond. For a moment, he thought he would mention it to his brothers, but then he shrugged his shoulders and strolled back to rejoin them.

"Who wants to go up to the pond with me?" he asked. Howard made a face, and Ed looked non-committal.

"Oh, well," Bert said, rummaging among the duffle for his fishing tackle, "then I'll go myself."

"Better take the map and a compass," Ed suggested. "It looks to me as if the trail isn't very clear." He reached in his pocket and handed the two items to Bert, who accepted them reluctantly, convinced that he could find the way by himself. Then, with a wave of the hand, he started into the brush, first stopping at the edge of the clearing to take a compass bearing.

The path was hard to follow, harder than he had thought. In the thick brush it was hot, and the flies were troublesome. Every now and then, a blackened log across the trail reminded him of the hazard of forest fire, and he involuntarily reached into his pocket to make sure that his matches were safely enclosed in their waterproof container. Try as he would, he kept wandering away from the brook; once, sweating and panting, he lost the trail for more than fifteen minutes, but finally picked it up again.

Ridge followed ridge; false summit followed false summit. Each time Bert crested a rise, he looked in vain for the pond. Still he kept on going until lengthening shadows convinced him that it was growing late. Reluctantly, he pulled out the map and compass and laid them on the ground. He turned the map until the north arrow, printed on one margin, coincided with the north arrow on his compass. He knelt to look at the result, and whistled in amazement. The pond lay due east of the river; and for some time, he had been traveling northeast. He was miles away from camp. Unless he was very lucky, he would have to spend the night in the woods. He let out a long sigh, consulted the map and compass once more, and swung around to begin the long trek back to camp.

It was dusk, but no cooler, as Bert dropped down again toward the brook. Before he knew it, he was knee-deep in a marsh, wallowing from hummock to hummock, and occasionally dropping waist-deep in icy water. He had a brief moment of panic before he collected his thoughts and gruffly said out loud to himself, "What're you getting so excited about? The worst that will happen is that you'll spend the night out in the woods. In the morning you can get back to camp again."

It seemed to Bert, as he struggled wearily along,

that the swamp was miles across. Once or twice he stopped to rest in tiny groves of swamp balsam, and the thought crossed his mind that he ought to make camp where he was, but he kept doggedly on. The more he traveled at night, he reminded himself, the less he would have to do in the morning.

Finally, his tired feet came out on harder ground. In the dim light, he could see that he was on an old logging road, and the luminous dial of the compass showed him that he was traveling in the right direction. It was an effort to move his feet, but he kept on plugging along. Once he heard the snort of a startled deer, and then a crashing in the underbrush. Off to his left, he could hear the tinkling of the brook as it dropped slowly down to join the main stream.

And then, as he rounded a corner, he saw ahead of him the glimmer of a campfire and heard the sound of voices. It took him a moment to adjust himself to this new discovery, but finally his tired eyes focused on the scene. Two men were squatting on either side of the fire. Bert's heart leaped. He was about to rush forward, but some primitive instinct warned him to stop and to listen. Though the fire was perhaps a hundred feet away, he could hear the sound of voices. There was something familiar about those voices; and, in a moment, he knew what it was.

"The Wallaces!" he whispered to himself. "They're right on our trail." He looked around him, searching for another path. There was none. Then defiance flooded into his veins, he set his jaw grimly, and reached a decision. He would creep up closer and hear what they were saying. Slowly, very carefully, he crawled into the thick underbrush, moving less than a foot every few minutes. He would lift each twig aside so as not to make any noise. Once a branch snapped, and he stopped stock still, but the men around the fire continued their conversation. He was getting closer now, and the saplings were thinning out a little.

"It's a cinch from now on," Bert assured himself, and took a step forward. His right foot went out from under him, and he fell to the ground amid a crash of snapping twigs.

A rough voice called, "Who's that?" and as Bert scrambled frantically to his feet and wheeled to run, he caught a glimpse of Tom Wallace's grizzled face.

CHAPTER SIXTEEN

A SKY-BORNE FRIEND

In that first moment of panic, Bert had the feeling that he was trapped. His first impulse was to run wildly off into the underbrush, but this was succeeded by the realization that now, more than ever, he must move quickly. The flickering light of the fire, in back of him, picked out the outline of a little grove of balsam just ahead. He could see the round beam of a flashlight penetrating the underbrush, as he tiptoed ahead and then crawled beneath the pungent, close-lying branches. The ground was thick with pine needles, sending their sharp odor into his nostrils. Off behind him, he could hear a crashing in the brush as he crawled on his stomach. Suddenly the ground dropped away in front of him, and he sailed out into space.

I'm done for, he thought for a frantic second, but then the boughs of another balsam received him, softly cushioning his fall and letting him down to solid ground again. Behind him, he could faintly see the ledge from which he had tumbled. The grayish rock, higher up, gave way to black space; and, in that second, he realized that he was looking into a cave. Needles, ripped from the balsam in his fall, prickled against the back of his neck and clung clammily to his damp shoulder blades. He let himself carefully to the ground, and crawled back into the hole.

Over the thudding noise of his pounding heart, he heard behind him a crashing in the forest, and then the gruff sound of Tom Wallace's voice. A dazzling light illuminated the area just in front of him. With Tom was Alan, and the two of them were arguing.

"I tell you, Dad," came Alan's high-pitched voice, "that must have been one of the Walton boys, sneaking up to spy on us. And if we could catch him—" He cackled, and the noise of his laughter was blood-curdling.

"Don't be a fool, son," came Tom Wallace's deeper voice. "That was a bear, I'll stake money on it." The flashlight beam flickered down, and came to rest on a small tree less than two feet in front of the cavern where Bert was crouching.

"See there!" he said triumphantly. "Claw marks on the tree! That was a bear, and not one of those doggoned kids. Bet if we looked, we'd still find 'em camped down at the clearing."

"Yeah, but—" protested Alan, still skeptical, to judge from the tone of his voice. "Shouldn't we keep on looking? If we can catch one of those fellows away from the others, we can hold onto him for a while and tie up the whole trip."

"That's right," agreed the elder Wallace, "but they're too smart. We'll just have to try something else. One of 'em is sure to do something foolish sooner or later. Remember how we caught the boy up in the old mine?"

"Sure do," agreed Alan, "and for a while, I thought we'd won."

The older man chuckled grimly. "They licked us that time and they took our mine away from us. But we'll get even. Just leave it to me. We'll get even."

The flashlight beam suddenly lifted, and there was a crackling in the brush as the Wallaces retreated. Bert let out his breath with a whooshing sound, and sat back in the darkness to think. He waited until five minutes had elapsed on the luminous dial of his watch before he cautiously struck a match and looked around him. A little spring trickled out of one corner, some soft grass grew on the ground; and, all in all, it was as snug a place as a boy could ask.

"Gee, I feel tired," he said to himself, and stretched out his arms to yawn. He leaned against one of the rock walls and tried to collect his thoughts. Should he try to go on that night, or should he wait until morning? If he went on, he might alarm the Wallaces again. If he waited until morning, he could get away quietly at dawn, while they were still sleeping, but while he could see. The choice was obvious. He stretched out full length, pillowed his head on one arm, and dropped off to sleep. Several times during the night, he awoke with a start. The ground was chilly under him, and outside in the trees, he could hear the faint dripping of dew. Finally exhaustion overcame him, and he slept.

In the faint light of dawn, he woke again. A gray light outlined the dripping tops of the trees and there was a faint stirring of wind, but not another sound. Very carefully, he crawled out from his cave and stood up, listening. Apparently the Wallaces were still asleep. Very well, he'd get away before they woke. Beyond him the ground dropped off again in another shelving ledge. Quietly but quickly, he made his way to the ledge and slid down. Now he was completely out of sight, and he could move more rapidly.

The stream still tinkled away, off to his left, and in places its banks were almost open. Bert was ravenously hungry now; he searched his pockets for some food, and was rewarded with a wilted piece of chocolate. Even that morsel gave him strength for the rest of the trip, and he moved steadily down the brook.

Before he reached the clearing, he scented the campfire. Wisps of smoke drifted off into the woods, and Bert breathed in the acrid odor, confident that he would be back at camp soon. But the wind was blowing harder now, and the campsite was farther away than he had thought. Finally, however, he parted one last clump of saplings and looked out into the swale. A big fire was snapping and crackling beside the tent; Howie and Ed were busy at their camp duties. He opened his mouth to yell; but, instead, tiptoed quietly up. He stuck out a hand and tapped Howard on the shoulder.

"Excuse me, mister, but have you seen a couple of Walton boys?" he said with a grin.

Howard jumped, whirled around, and let out a yell. "Bert!" he shouted. "Bert! You're back!" Ed flung his arm around Bert, and the three boys danced around in a circle.

"Good grief," Ed finally said, "we thought you were lost forever. We couldn't hope to find you in the darkness, but we were going to make a try at it this morning."

Bert rapidly told his brothers what had happened, and had to laugh at the serious expression on their faces.

"Aw, don't worry," he concluded. "I heard 'em say that they wouldn't try anything as long as we stuck together. Anyway I'm not afraid of those fellows. And now, me for some breakfast!"

He eagerly sipped a mug of scalding hot cocoa,

spooned up some oatmeal, and settled down to work in earnest on some bacon and powdered eggs. Even the powdered eggs, which he ordinarily disliked, tasted good to him. He finally sat back, with a satisfied sigh, and contemplated the new day ahead. After a moment or two of thought, he reached for a potful of steaming water, poured a little into a basin, and vigorously scrubbed his face.

"I never thought that just washing my face could make me feel so good," he said.

"And what now?" Howard asked, leaning forward eagerly. The night's experiences, somehow, had made him a bit of a hero, Bert realized. He pulled the crumpled map from his pocket and scanned it.

"Well," he indicated, "we can go down to Marsh Pond, that's about ten miles downstream, and hole up for the night. That'll put us a little ahead of the Wallaces. Maybe we can take a swim, if we get there early enough, and rest up for the night."

Half an hour later, with Bert relaxing in the center of the canoe and Howard taking his place in the bow, they were out in the main current again and moving swiftly along. The rains of the day before had swollen the river, and even the small rapids were so well covered that they simply shot down through them without using a setting pole, or scarcely slowing their speed. Gradually, as Bert dozed and time passed, the current slowed until they were

Howard Took Bert's Place in the Bow

paddling along through a wide, meandering still water that opened, at the farther end, into a broad, wind-rippled pond.

"Marsh Pond," Bert heard Howard say, and then he dropped off to sleep again. He did not awake until the canoe grated on a sandy beach. He raised himself on one elbow to look out across the water. The shores were far away. In the middle of the lake two loons were floating on the waves, calling to one another in high, cackling voices. Otherwise the silence was complete. It was like Mud Pond, only on a larger scale; and, by common consent, none of the boys spoke as they quietly unloaded their canoe and prepared to pitch camp.

Out of the north, suddenly, came a high-pitched, droning sound. It grew louder and louder. Bert recognized it instantly and ran out on the shore, shielding his eyes. High overhead, darting in and out of puffy cumulus clouds, there was a plane. As he watched, it began a long glide down toward the lake.

"Look!" he said, nudging his brothers, and pointing at the descending ship. It continued to come down until he could see the pontoons underneath. Finally it lit as gently as a feather on the waves, swung around, and began to taxi toward them.

"He sees us!" Howard yelled, and Bert felt the sting of his younger brother's hand on his shoulder blades. In his own excitement, Bert waded out into the water, knee deep, ignoring the chill that soaked into his boots and numbed his legs. The plane came closer and closer, its propeller roaring, until it was less than a hundred feet offshore. Then the propeller spun more slowly, choked, and stopped. The door of the cabin swung open, and a rubber boat was tossed out to land with a splash on the water. Two legs dropped down on the pontoon, followed by the rest of a man's body. As Bert stared out across the water, a curly-haired young man with an engaging grin waved at him and said, "Hi."

Before Bert could reply, the visitor had settled down in his little boat, and was swiftly paddling ashore. He leaped out on the beach, Bert splashing alongside him, and stuck out his hand. Howard and Ed, meanwhile, had run down to the shore line and were staring at the stranger, who nodded briskly to them before turning to talk again to Bert.

"I'm Pete Harvey," he said. "A private pilot. I take fishing parties in to these lakes. I saw your canoe on the shore there, and I thought I'd come down to see how you're getting along."

"Well, gee, come on up on shore and have a cup of cocoa or coffee," Bert urged him.

Harvey unlimbered his long legs and strode into the little clearing where the duffle bags were piled. "Got an ax?" he asked, and Bert handed him his own, light-bladed, Hudson's Bay ax. Harvey loped off into the brush, and could be heard chopping vigorously. In a few minutes, he came back with an armful of branches, and a length or two of logs. These he piled in a pyramid, jammed some birch bark underneath, pulled a match from his trousers, struck it and put the tiny flame under the pyramid. In a moment, the fire was crackling gayly.

"I don't suppose you fellows are tired of fish yet?" he said inquiringly as he sat down on a log.

"Well, no—" said Bert hesitantly, "but even if we were, what could we do about it? Strangle a moose with our bare hands?"

"I wouldn't advise that, son," said the guide, "but if one of you will paddle out to my plane, I think you might find a little steak in a box full of ice, under the seat of the cockpit."

"Wow!" yelled Bert. "Lead me to it!" He sprinted for the shore, and made it in a dead heat with Howard. Together, the two of them splashed out to the plane and climbed aboard. Standing on the pontoon, Bert poked his head in through the door. At other times, being mechanically minded, he would have been interested in the array of instruments on the panel. Now, all he was interested in was the thought of steak. Under the pilot's seat, he could see a heavy box. Grunting a little, he dragged it out and lifted the lid. There, wrapped in paper, was some meat.

He stuffed it inside his shirt and dropped back into the boat.

"Boy, it's certainly going to be good to eat something besides fish!" He sighed as he dipped the tiny paddle into the water. Both he and Howard leaped out at the same time, dragged the rubber boat a short distance up on the beach, and then sprinted for the fire.

"Here it is, Mr. Harvey!" Bert said, reaching inside his shirt. Through its wrappings, the steak felt cool. The pilot reached for a frying pan, put it on to heat, and then raised his eyebrows inquiringly. "But where's the butter?" he asked. Bert rummaged through the nearest duffle bag, and then handed him the butter tin. The pilot scooped out a huge chunk, dropped it in the frying pan, and let it sizzle. A moment later, he dropped in a hunk of steak, and its seductive aroma spread in a thick cloud around the fire.

Bert closed his eyes to savor the aroma, then opened them again as Harvey pulled out a hunting knife and began to carve the steak into fragments. Howard had assembled the knives, forks, dishes, and Harvey lifted out a chunk of steak and dropped it into Bert's plate, following suit with the others. Bert thought, as he lifted a piece of the meat to his mouth, that he never had tasted anything so good.

"Boy, are we glad you came along," said Howard,

his mouth half full. "With or without the steak," he hastily amended. Harvey threw back his head and laughed.

"Well, I know how it is when you've been out for a long time," he said. "A little meat makes a nice substitute for fish. Of course, if you get tired of fish, you can always kill a spruce grouse—we call 'em *fool hens* up here—for a substitute. They're so tame you can walk right up on 'em."

"Right now I'll settle for steak," Bert said with a heartfelt sigh. He wasn't hinting, but Harvey promptly fished another piece of meat from the frying pan, commenting that there was plenty more. After dinner was over, he helped with the dishwashing. Bert noticed how efficient he was at this distasteful job.

"I always do the dishes right after a meal." He grinned. "It's twice as tough to do 'em an hour later."

Bert, feeling better fed than ever before, was inclined to agree with him.

CHAPTER SEVENTEEN

FORCED LANDING

"Chow down!" This cry, punctuated by the sound of a spoon being beaten against a pan, woke Bert from the most satisfying sleep he had enjoyed since their expedition started. He rolled over in his sleeping bag and looked out the door. As he had suspected, Pete Harvey was already at work. The fire was crackling; a kettle at one side was sending up a cloud of steam, and griddle cakes were browning in the frying pan. Bert climbed out of the tent. Harvey smiled at him, and handed him a plateful of griddle cakes, already drenched with syrup and flanked by four strips of crisp bacon.

"Sure tastes good!" Bert acknowledged gratefully as he picked up a fork and sat down to relish one of the best breakfasts he had ever tasted. Howard and Ed, he noticed, were clambering sleepily from their bags. After everyone was served, Harvey himself filled a plate with food.

Bert, meanwhile, walked down to the lake for a pailful of water. Without being asked to, he collected the dishes and methodically washed and dried them.

179

"And now," he said, contemplating with satisfaction his own efficiency, "what do we do today? Keep on paddling or take a rest?"

"Maybe I can answer that question for you," Harvey said, looking across the fire at Bert and his completely relaxed brothers. "Perhaps you'd like to make a flight with me today."

"Boy, would we!" said Howard. Bert looked at Ed, and his older brother nodded approvingly.

"Why, sure," Ed said, approvingly. "I guess we can take a day off. Who knows, we might see something."

"Just what I was thinking," commented Bert. "We might even see the Wallaces."

"And who are the Wallaces?" inquired Harvey. As Bert unreeled the story, he could see dawning interest in Harvey's eyes.

"Sounds mighty interesting," the pilot finally said. "Tell you what, bring your fishing tackle. We'll fly in to Grampus Pond for landlocked salmon fishing, and buzz over the spot where you saw the Wallaces. We can tell if they've moved on, or if they're still there."

"But will the plane carry all of us?" asked Bert.

"Sure," said Harvey, gesturing expansively. "It's a four-seater. If we get some of the duffle ashore that I packed into the fuselage, we'll have no trouble at all."

"Okay," said Harvey, when his duffle was ashore. "I can row two of you out in one trip, and then come back for the other one." The shuttle trip was quickly negotiated. The boys clambered into the cabin of the plane, Ed and Howard in the rear seats, by mutual consent; Bert in one of the front seats. The pilot lingered for a moment on the pontoon, twisted a nozzle that deflated the rubber boat, and then passed it up to Bert before he clambered into the plane himself.

"Everything looks okay," he said, glancing quickly at the instrument panel. "Let's go." He stepped on the starter, and the propeller spun over, then quickened, and the plane began to vibrate. Harvey looked out ahead and pulled the throttle forward. He pulled the control stick back a little, and the plane skimmed ahead. Again Harvey pulled back on the stick, and they were bouncing along the tops of the waves. As Bert looked out, he could feel the familiar sinking sensation in his stomach, and then they were air-borne. Harvey eased off on the stick as they climbed. Soon the lake was too far below them for individual waves to be distinguished, and off in the distance the bulk of Mt. Katahdin, blue in the morning sunshine, dominated the landscape.

Bert pressed his nose against the window and stared upstream. He could see every bend in the river down which they had so laboriously traveled.

Off in the distance, half a dozen lakes sparkled. Harvey made a gesture toward one of them, and into the upper end of which a wide, calm river flowed.

"Grampus Pond!" he shouted. "That's where we're bound." Bert turned around, nudged his brothers, and pointed through the broad windshield toward the pond, which was coming closer and closer. The plane began to lose altitude, then dropped into a steep glide, leveled out and bounced twice before it finally began to run smoothly along the waters of Grampus Pond.

"Well, that's it," the pilot said to him. "Now, for some landlocked salmon." From beneath his seat, he pulled a sturdy, steel rod, to which a line and a glittering spoon lure already were attached. He leaned over, swung open the door, crawled past Bert and dropped lightly down on the pontoon. The reel whirred and hummed as he made a long cast, and the spoon plunked into the water with a splash. As he reeled it in, there was a tug on the line. "Got one!" he said, and tightened the line. The fish fought grimly, but finally Harvey drew it alongside the pontoon. In the green water the silver-sided salmon looked pale, but when Harvey finally lifted it out, Bert could see a faint reddish tinge to its scales. Harvey whipped a knife from his pocket, deftly slit the fish's stomach, and cleaned it in the cold water before handing it up to Bert.

"Want to try?" he asked, and Bert dropped to the pontoon beside him. His extra weight tipped the plane a little, and he could feel the water sloshing against his soles. He gratefully accepted the rod from Harvey, and made a preliminary cast. Immediately, he felt the impact as a hungry fish took the lure. This fish bore deep down for a time, then came out on the surface, seeming to dance on his tail as he shook his head in a vain effort to throw loose the hook. Finally he subsided into a sulk far down, and the rod bent as Bert pumped him to the surface.

Harvey bent down and stuck his finger under the salmon's gills. "Nice fish," he commented, as he flipped the gasping salmon clear of the water. "Now, let's go ashore and let the other boys do some fishing at the mouth of the river." He climbed back into the cabin and began to taxi toward the river's mouth.

"Okay," he called into the back of the cabin, "let's have the rubber boat and a new bottle of carbon dioxide. There's one tucked away back there." Ed handed forward these two items, the boat floppy and inert, and Harvey quickly attached the bottle of carbon dioxide. To Bert, he said, "Crawl out, and lay the boat on the edge of the pontoon. Then just turn that nozzle, and she'll inflate."

Bert complied. He jumped as he turned the nozzle, for there was a loud hiss of air, and then the boat quickly began to inflate until he was able to nudge it off the pontoon and into the water, where it floated free. "Let's go!" he called into the cabin, and the other boys crawled out. There was a splash, as Harvey threw the anchor out of the window alongside his seat, as a guarantee that the plane would stay put if a sudden wind came up, and then they began to paddle ashore in relays.

As Howard and Ed fished at the river's mouth, Bert and Harvey started a roaring fire. Harvey had brought a huge kettle ashore from the plane. Into this he dipped water, and then threw in a handful of salt. When the water came to a boil, he tossed into its bubbles the two fish they had caught. "Makes 'em nice and flaky," he said. "A change from fried or broiled fish." He picked out a piece of pinkish salmon, dropped it on a slab of birch bark, and handed it to Bert. "Eat it with your hands," he said. Bert did, and agreed at once that it was delicious.

Up from the river's mouth came Howard and Ed a moment later, staggering under the weight of half a dozen fish. These they dropped by the fire, then sat down to gorge on salmon.

The sun rode high in the noontime sky when Harvey glanced at his watch. "Guess we might as well get over and see what's happened to your friends, the Wallaces," he suggested. "Locate them on the map for me."

Bert pointed out, as best he could, the little pond near which he had seen the Wallaces. "I think they must have camped in a shanty clearing near by," he said. "Probably there was lumbering in there at some time in the past."

"I've got it located," Harvey said. "We'll give it a buzz and see what happens."

In a plane, as opposed to a canoe, it took them only ten minutes to cover the distance to the area where Bert had seen the Wallaces the night before. The plane circled round and round, and its droning noise echoed back from the rock-rimmed hills, but there was no sign of a campfire, of any evidence of campers. Finally Bert nudged the pilot. Below him, he had recognized the ledges where he had hidden, and, back of them, a little clearing. He pointed down, and Harvey nodded his head. The plane dived down on the clearing, and banked so that Bert was looking directly into it. A pang of disappointment shot through his heart. There was nobody there.

"They've moved," he shouted into the pilot's ear. "I guess we might as well go back to camp." Harvey held up his right thumb and finger, and circled them in the familiar pilot's gesture of acknowledgement, then took the plane into one more dive over the clearing. Bert strained his eyes until they ached, but all he could see was the blackened evidence of a former campfire, and no evidence at all that the

Wallaces were still there. Again, the horizon leveled out, and Bert could look out through the bluish air to Katahdin, so magnificent in the distance. At its base, a great river spilled down in a creamy flood, and then the forest floor flattened to form a green carpet for this most impressive of the eastern mountains.

As Bert looked out, fascinated by what he saw in the distance, the engine gave a warning cough. He turned his head, and Harvey, a puzzled frown on his face, began to fiddle with the controls. The engine roared, sputtered, and then roared again as Harvey tinkered away. Then suddenly the engine stopped completely, and Bert could hear the whistling of the wind outside as they silently began to lose altitude. Ahead of them was a big lake, its surface dappled by whitecaps. He turned around to look at the white faces of his two brothers.

"We're going to have to make a forced landing," Harvey said quietly. "Must be that the gas line's plugged. Just strap yourself in good and solid, but be ready to get out if we start to sink after we hit. This has happened to me before, so don't worry."

The words were reassuring, but the tone of Harvey's voice was not. The forest beneath was coming closer and closer, but so, also, was the lake. Then they were skimming along over the treetops. Bert looked at Harvey, who was pulling back on the stick.

Just that last effort was enough. They cleared a cluster of pine and soared out over the water, then dropped rapidly and landed with a wracking splash that twisted the plane and shook Bert as if a giant terrier had picked him up and worried him like a bone. Then they were floating, and on Harvey's face was a happy smile.

"We made it," he said softly. "Nothing to worry about now except to find ourselves a place to camp." Bert exhaled his breath and took a lungful of fresh air. Just being alive seemed somehow more wonderful to him than it ever had before. He glanced back at Ed, who was grinning, and at Howard, whose eyes were still wide with the wonder of the experience.

"Okay, let's get ashore," said Harvey, gesturing to the right. Just a few hundred feet away was a sandy beach and a pine-covered island. It seemed less than ten minutes, but must have been double that time, when they finally paddled ashore in the rubber boat and began to make camp. Night was dropping, and Harvey turned over the task of the evening meal to Bert while he tinkered with the engine of the plane. He carefully removed the fuel line and blew through it; he worked on the cylinders; and, finally, his face smudged but smiling, came back to report that they could take off again early the next morning.

"I found the trouble," he said, "and now I'm ready for some food and a good balsam bed. Let's eat!" Nobody argued with his conclusions as the boys joined him around the fire.

CHAPTER EIGHTEEN

UNWELCOME VISITORS

The spluttering roar of the airplane motor echoed from the tree-hung shores of the pond. It was a reassuring sound, and the day was a reassuring one with puffy cumulus clouds and a faint breeze ruffling the water. That would make a take-off easier, Bert reflected. In a few minutes everything had been loaded, the boat was deflated, and Bert slammed shut the cabin door.

"Everything's hunky-dory!" he heard Harvey shout above the motor noise, and then the plane began to taxi. Perhaps ten minutes later, Bert felt a nudge from the pilot and looked down to see the sinuous bends of the river below. They began to drop again toward the little pond formed by a widening of the stream, and skittered across its rippled surface. The plane settled down in the water, let out one final roar as Harvey gunned the motor for a test, and slid smoothly in toward the shallows. Bert stretched his arms, grinned widely, and said, "Home again."

"Looks just the same as it did—" Bert began, and then he focused his eyes on the campsite. Something seemed wrong. Either the duffle bags had been moved, or else someone had been prying into their belongings. And the tent—the tent sagged wearily as if, perhaps, one or two of the guy ropes had been cut.

"Hey!" he shouted, swinging around to look at his brothers, and he realized that they, too, knew that something was wrong. Very quickly he pulled out the rubber boat, inflated it, and paddled ashore with Howard.

"Bring the others in," he flung over his shoulder as he started up the bank at a run. He dropped to his knees beside the pile of duffle. One or two bags had been tossed to one side; from a rip in a third bag, flour had seeped out. Bert jumped up again and sprinted to the tent. It, too, was ripped, and two of the guy ropes had been pulled loose. Inside, feathers had spilled from the sleeping bags, almost as if some animal had been rooting around.

"Bear," Bert said to himself breathlessly. "I'll bet a dollar, bear have been around here searching for food." He pulled his head out of the tent and strode down to the shore line just as Howie, Ed, and Harvey slid up to the sandy bank.

"We've had visitors," he said, relishing the wide-eyed expression on Howard's face and the sudden narrowing of Ed's blue eyes. "And they did a little damage."

"Bear," Said Bert, "Or So It Looks."

"Who?" asked Howard, his eyes darting about to take in the shambles.

"Bear," said Bert, "or so it looks. They must have been after our food. They got into the flour; some of the sugar is gone, and our supplies are pretty much in a mess."

Harvey, his sleeves rolled up to his elbows, brushed past Bert and the other brothers, and began a swift inspection of the damage. He lingered over the duffle bags, peered into the tent, and walked slowly around the edge of the clearing, stopping to stare at the ground.

"Come here, boys," he called, and Bert led the little procession to his side. He pointed down at the ground. There was a dusty spot, where partridge apparently had been sunning themselves.

"That doesn't look like bear to me," he indicated. "That looks like the track of a two-footed animal. Maybe a rat, a human one, that is."

Bert felt a slow surge of anger. "You're right, Mr. Harvey," he admitted. "And I know who the rat is. It's one of the Wallaces."

"This close to us?" gasped Howard, and Bert could see the paleness of his younger brother's normally ruddy face.

"Yeah," Bert said bitterly. "They must have thought they could wreck our camp and make us think that bear did it. And," he turned his head to look back at the wreckage of the duffle, "they did a pretty good job of it, pretty recently. We must've scared 'em off when we came in to land." He clenched his fists and walked slowly back to the duffle.

A closer inspection revealed that fully half of their food supplies were ruined. Cans had been ripped open; jam mingled with woolen socks; cocoa had sifted through underwear; sugar stuck to flannel shirts.

"What in the dickens are we going to do, Bert?" Howard inquired as he dropped on his knees beside his older brother.

"Well, either we'll get along on mighty short rations for the rest of the trip, or we'll have to turn back," Bert said grimly. He looked at Ed, who nodded his agreement. As he pawed through the wreckage, he noticed that Harvey was strolling toward them, and then he felt the touch of a hand on his shoulder.

"Don't take it too hard, kid," the pilot said gruffly. "You're not too far from Eagle Lake, and the ranger down there is a good friend of mine. He always keeps a stock of food on hand; I'll have him lend you some, and I'll fly up to the village and replace what you take."

"I can't thank you enough," Bert said quietly. "And I'm not going to try to. Right now, I'm going hunting."

"Hunting?" inquired Ed, looking up at him from a crouching position. "Hunting for what?"

"For rats," Bert said grimly. "Two-legged ones." Anticipating the protest he knew would follow, he added hastily, "This is a job for one person. It's a job of tracking. I'll take the map and the compass, and I'll keep track of the time. Maybe, if I'm lucky, I can sneak up on the Wallaces and find out what they plan to do next."

Before his brothers could protest, he was at the edge of the clearing, intently examining the footprints in the dust. Then he pushed through the fringing barrier of balsam and found himself alone in the woods. The tracking was hard work; now and then grass was bent, as if a heavy-footed person had walked that way; once or twice twigs were freshly broken. In one tiny marsh, the footprints stood out clearly. Just one of the Wallaces had taken part in the destructive expedition, for only one set of prints could be found. As he stopped for a moment, he heard the roar of an airplane motor. He realized that Harvey was leaving for Eagle Lake to talk to the ranger, to get them their food, and to keep his promise.

As the noise of the motor died away, Bert pushed ahead. On his forehead he could feel tiny, cool drops of perspiration. He reached in his pocket, pulled out the bottle of fly dope, uncorked it and spread some of the greasy mixture on his face. It was growing more humid, and the flies would be bad. Ahead of him, he could see the faint glimmer of water. He pushed through a screen of branches and out on the edge of a tiny pond. Across from him, something moved. He took a more careful look. It was a bull moose, scarcely two hundred feet away. Beside the bull, feeding placidly, was a cow moose, who raised her head once or twice and sniffed the air. From her lower lip hung a wreath of dripping water plants. The bull, apparently, was unaware that a human was anywhere around.

Bert felt a thrill of excitement. Heretofore, the moose he had seen were those viewed from a passing canoe. Except for the one bull that Jed had ridden ashore so spectacularly, he had never been really close to this monarch of the woods. He felt a sudden urge to get closer to the animal, to inspect him. Very slowly, he crept around the shore of the pond. Under his feet he felt the familiar sogginess of marsh grass. Once a twig cracked, and he froze in position as the moose lifted his head and stared intently around him. He was fairly close now, but the bull, apparently having satisfied his suspicions, had gone back to feeding again. His head was toward Bert, who counted the spikes on his antlers. Twenty points! That was a big moose.

Again Bert could feel the perspiration standing out on his forehead. He was excited and a little afraid. *Moose won't bother you,* he told himself. *They'll run from you.* And yet, there was the question in the back of his mind: *But will they?* Still he crept closer, until finally he was a scant twenty feet away from the feeding bull and his mate. The wind was blowing lightly from them toward him, so that they could not scent him. He was close enough, he told himself; yet he wanted to be still closer. He took one step forward. A dead branch cracked beneath his outstretched right foot. The bull moose raised his head; the cow stared at the intruder and then splashed noisily into deeper water. The bull emitted a sound that was halfway between a snort and a bellow, and then started for Bert.

"I'm caught," Bert said miserably. "This one is an exception to the rule. He's going to chase me. Maybe he's even mad, like the moose Jed told us about!"

He was running through the underbrush before he really knew what he was doing. A little distance behind him, too little, he could hear the crashing of the angered bull. He almost tripped as he shot a glance ahead, looking for a tree he could climb. The trees were all clean, tall maples and beech with no lower branches, but a few score feet ahead he could see a gnarled pine with low-growing branches.

It seemed to him that the moose was breathing down his neck as he lunged forward and began to scramble frantically up the trunk of the pine. There was a reverberating crash, and a vibration in the tree trunk, and he looked down. Ten feet below him, the bull had butted the pine with his antlers. Now he paced around and around the tree, occasionally snorting and pawing the ground. Bert looked at his watch. It was only eleven o'clock. He had plenty of time to wait, but if only that moose would go away! He shifted his perch and almost fell, but he shot out an arm and rescued himself in time. By wriggling, he finally got himself settled between a massive branch and the main trunk.

Hours passed, and still the moose refused to go away. Bert felt a gnawing sensation in his stomach, and his watch confirmed what he felt. It was long after lunchtime. He managed to break loose a rotten branch and threw it down on the now quiescent bull, but instead of chasing the animal away, this only seemed to enrage him. Again and again the bull hit the tree trunk a shattering blow with his head before he resumed his uneasy movements around its base. *Maybe he'll stay here all night,* Bert thought numbly. He did not like to entertain such fears, but time was still slipping past. In the west, the sun was beginning to drop out of sight beyond a ridge. Oily-looking clouds were drifting across its face, warning signals of an approaching storm.

Whanggg! the scream of a bullet woke Bert from his reverie. It was repeated twice. The bull snorted uneasily, wheeled in the direction of the sound, and then dove clumsily into the underbrush. Bert could see him crash through the trees for a distance, and then could follow his flight by the swaying of the saplings. *Who but the Wallaces would have a gun?* He resigned himself to the worst, and climbed slowly down the trunk to the ground. His stiffened legs would not let him move very rapidly. He sat down amid the fragrant, brownish needles, and stretched his legs out in front of him. Even the Wallaces could do him no more harm than the bull moose would have. Not far distant, he could hear a faint *crack,* as someone moved stealthily. He fixed his eyes on the trees, waiting for someone to come through them. A faint and husky "Hi," from behind him made his heart jump. He sprang to his feet and looked, not into the face of Tom Wallace, but into the ruddy face and white-bearded cheeks of a total stranger.

"Hello, sonny," the stranger said quietly, and stuck out his hand. "You in trouble?"

"I was," said Bert, returning the handshake, "but you saved me, and I can't thank you enough."

"Oh, that's all right," the stranger said, parting his lips in a smile that disclosed snaggleteeth. "I was just a-wanderin' around when I heard that moose snortin'. It's agin the law to kill 'em, but I figgered he was a bad 'un, and had someone treed, so I just fired over his head. That did it."

"It sure did," agreed Bert, inspecting the stranger more closely. His rescuer wore a deer-hide suit, with thongs replacing buttons. He wore no hat on his shock of white hair. On his feet he had moccasins. The gun he carried was an old-fashioned, lever-action rifle. It sat lightly in the crook of his arm.

"Do you live around here?" Bert finally asked curiously. The stranger grinned again.

"Yup," he said succinctly, "this is my home. Come along with me, and I'll show you where I stay." He led the way, padding silently on his moccasins, back through the trees until they came out on a faint path. A few hundred feet ahead was a clearing; and, in the clearing, a crude tepee made of birch bark and logs, with earth piled up around its base.

"Welcome to the hermit's house," the stranger said expansively, flinging out one arm as Bert crouched down to crawl inside the tepee.

"Gee, are you really a hermit?" Bert asked breathlessly. His host had climbed in, and was sitting opposite him on a crudely carved chair. A fire, on a pile of rocks in the center of the tepee, sent a flickering column of smoke toward a hole in the roof.

"That's right, sonny," the white-bearded stranger said. "Name's Belton. Donald Belton. I've been livin' up in here for fifteen years, mostly by myself. But I'm always glad to welcome strangers." He hauled forward a kettle, set it on the coals; and, in a moment, the savory smell of warming soup permeated the tepee.

CHAPTER NINETEEN

THE BEAVER HOUSE

Very swiftly, between spoonfuls of soup, Bert had told the story of the Wallaces to the hermit. The old man listened reflectively, never once interrupting to ask a question. When Bert finished, however, the hermit laid down his spoon and soup bowl with a clatter. He hunched forward, resting his elbows on his knees, and looked intently at Bert.

"That's not right," he muttered. "That's not right at all."

"Of course it isn't right," Bert agreed, though somewhat puzzled by the hermit's reaction. "But there isn't much we can do about it until we get to Eagle Lake."

"Yet you don't even know if these people will go through Eagle Lake," broke in the hermit, more impatiently. "Mebbe they'll go around through some of the side ponds. Did you think of that?"

"Golly, no!" Bert said, struck with the idea. "But what can we do to head 'em off?"

"I'll tell you what we can do!" the hermit said, and Bert stared at him as he smacked a fist into the palm of his other hand. "We can join up forces and

201

track 'em down!"

"You mean you'll travel with us for a while?"
Bert asked, still dumbfounded.

"You bet I will!" said the hermit, his brown eyes
sending off sparks. "I've lived up here peaceful-like
for too many years, and I don't want outlaws run-
nin' around. From what you tell me, these Wallaces
are outlaws. There's only one thing to do. Get rid
of 'em!"

"But I'm afraid they're carrying guns with them,"
Bert remonstrated. "I don't want you to get into a
shooting scrape with 'em. It wouldn't be fair to ask
you to take a chance like that."

"Don't worry," said the hermit, sitting down
again. "I've got a scheme. I'll smoke 'em out, believe
me, I will."

"Boy, that's wonderful!" Bert cried. He sprang to
his feet and ducked his head to crawl out through
the entrance of the tepee. The hermit followed him,
clutching two blankets.

"I know exactly where your camp is," the hermit
said, and plunged directly into the tangled woods.
Bert found it hard to keep up with him. *The man
may be old,* he thought to himself as he panted
across swamps and through the brush, *but he's still
perfectly spry.*

Ahead of him through the trees, Bert saw the
clearing in which their camp was located, and could

catch a glimpse of his brothers as they moved around
the embers of the noonday campfire. The watch on
his wrist told him it was three o'clock, and he wondered dimly whether they would have to spend the
night where they were. Then he was in the clearing,
introducing the hermit to his brothers. He chuckled
to see Howard's amazed expression, and the quizzical
look on Ed's face. Both of them were obviously de-
lighted that Belton was to accompany them.

"Well, what do you think?" he asked the hermit.
"Should we camp here tonight, or can we go on a
little way downstream?"

"I think we might as well go down to the campin'
place below Moose Rapids," the hermit said, after
giving the matter due thought. "I got a hunch those
fellers have moved on back to Grouse Pond; that's
not far from the river, close enough so they can still
keep an eye on you."

"Okay," said Bert, heaving a pack to his shoulders
and carrying it down to the canoe. Soon, all the
duffle was loaded, and then the problem arose. Could
they transport the hermit in their canoe? Belton
solved this question in his own way.

"I don't use the river much," he explained. "I've
got some private paths down along the shore. I'll
walk, and you just carry my blankets. Moose Rapids
is about four miles below, and the campsite's on the
pond at the other end of the portage. I'll meet you

there." With a wave of his hand, he disappeared
into the forest as Bert dug his paddle into the water
and the downstream trip was resumed.

The pond beside which they had camped gave
way to a winding stream once more, to a series of
short rapids, and then to Moose Rapids itself. From
a distance, Bert could hear the ominous thunder of
the roaring waters. As the canoe rounded a bend, he
could see how the river gathered itself together and
leaped down over cascades and boulders, in a massive demonstration of its force. Mist floated in the
air above the rapids, and tiny water birds darted in
and out of it. Obviously it was not a rapids to be run
in a canoe. He could feel the pull of the current,
and then a few strokes of his paddle, helped by Ed
in the stern, sent them darting up to a muddy bank.
On the shore a battered signboard, long since ren-
dered indistinct by wind and weather, showed the
beginning of the portage.

Grunting under the strain of the canoe, Bert began to wish that the trip around the rapids was
shorter. Actually, it was more than a mile, and he
was tired. Even worse, the inside of his right shoe
was rubbing a sore spot on his heel. He stopped,
once or twice, and even debated putting down the
canoe to apply a piece of adhesive tape or to adjust
his wrinkled sock, but, instead, he kept doggedly on.
Finally, he felt the resilience of meadow grass under

his shoes, and the glint of water just ahead. He swung the canoe to the ground, and looked around him. To his left, the creamy flow of the rapids eddied out into another widening of the river, much like the one on which they had camped yesterday. This, however, was a bigger pond. He wondered how the hermit would get across from the other side of the stream, and looked curiously upstream for a clue. Just then he saw the old man, balanced precariously on a slippery log, crossing at a point where the stream was narrowest. Once or twice Bert felt sure that Belton would slip and fall, but the hermit's sense of balance was miraculous. He made his way nimbly across the rocks on the same side of the stream as Bert, and then padded quietly down to join him just as Howard and Ed came struggling down through the last bouldery bit of the portage and dropped their loads with a grateful sigh.

"Nice little pond, here," the hermit said to Bert. "Lots of beaver. I trap here a lot." He gestured toward the pond. Out near its center Bert could see a dome-shaped structure of mud and branches. "Beaver house," said the hermit, anticipating his question. "They live in there. They get in under the water, and then there's space enough, with air, above the water line."

"Have you ever looked inside one of those beaver houses?" Bert asked curiously.

"Well, no," said the hermit, "but I generally set my traps at the entrance. They do say, in the old days when the Indians was raisin' trouble around here, some of the settlers escaped by swimmin' under water and hidin' inside the beaver houses until the Indians went away."

"Sounds fascinating," Bert said grudgingly. "But I don't think I'd like to try it." He swung on his heel, picked up an ax, and methodically began to chop wood for the supper fire. The hermit, meanwhile, borrowed Ed's fishing tackle, and went down the pond shore a short distance. He was back soon with three trout flopping from a rope stringer attached to his buckskin belt. After dinner as darkness settled down, Bert sat beside the fire with his brothers and talked idly with the hermit.

"What's your idea for fixing the Wallaces so they won't bother us any more?" he asked finally. The hermit put a finger to his lips.

"I ain't sayin' until I'm sure it works," he said. He pulled his finger from his lips and took a healthy swat at a black fly that had lit on the back of his neck.

"Better lend me some fly dope," he said. "I think this is going to be a bad night for flies." Bert handed him a bottle of the liquid, and the hermit smeared it generously on his face, yawning the while.

"I'm sleepy," he said, "and I'm goin' to bed. Anybody else tired?"

"All of us," answered Bert, and rose to his feet. Inside the tent, when he crawled through the doorway, the hermit was already asleep, snoring rhythmically.

In the morning, an unfamiliar aching sensation at the back of his right heel woke Bert from a sound sleep. Drowsily, he reached down to touch the spot. Pain shot through his foot, and he grunted between clenched teeth, then withdrew the leg from the sleeping bag to look at it. An angry-looking raw spot was visible where the skin had rubbed away. Even the application of a piece of sterile gauze and adhesive tape failed to stop the stinging, and the pressure of a shoe was almost unbearable.

"Guess I'll have to sit quiet for a day," he told his sober-faced brothers at breakfast. "This foot is killing me, and I don't think I'd better move until it heals a little."

"Gee, that sort of puts a crimp in our traveling," complained Howard, sympathy in his eyes. The hermit, who had been listening quietly, suddenly came over and sat down beside Bert.

"Don't let it worry you, sonny," he said comfortingly. "As a matter of fact, I'd like to take the other two boys and go lookin' for these Wallaces, just to see whether or not they're camped on the pond I told you about."

"Well, then, I'll stay here and hold down the camp," Bert said, much relieved at this solution to his problem. He sat back against a convenient log, and crossed his legs so as to keep the injured heel off the ground. The sun was bright, and he began to doze just as the hermit, Howard, and Ed started off in the woods. He waved to them, and then fell sound asleep.

Something, he never knew quite what, woke him from his sleep a little later. He stiffened as he heard the sound of unfamiliar voices. They were coming from behind him.

The Wallaces! he thought, chilled with apprehension. *And I'm here alone!*

He looked frantically about him for a hiding place. Out by the shore, the bank dropped steeply down to the pond. There was a little space between the water and the base of the bank. Half-hobbling, half-running, Bert slid over the edge of the bank and crouched close to it just as he heard Tom Wallace's familiar, hateful voice in the clearing.

"They're all gone!" he heard Wallace call out. "Don't know where, but this is our chance. We'll hide the food and burn up their tent. If that don't teach 'em a lesson, I don't know what will." He laughed, and the sound was bloodcurdling. In the clearing, Bert could hear Alan Wallace's grumbling voice, and his muscles tightened with anger and helplessness. There was not a thing he could do. If they would just go away without coming down to the pond!

Above his head he could hear a crackling sound, and then a dark, heavy column of smoke began to climb into the sky. That, he told himself, must be the tent. Quivering with rage and tension, he clenched his fists. For a moment he was tempted to leap up the bank and confront his enemies, but better judgment prevailed, and he remained quiet, hardly daring to breathe.

Again there came the sound of Tom Wallace's heavy guffaw, and, for a moment, silence. Bert crouched against the bank. Sand and mud trickled down his neck, but he was certain he had better not make a move.

"There's the canoe!" he suddenly heard the elder Wallace say. "Maybe we ought to go down and smash it so they can't use it again. Then we'll have 'em!"

What to do? Bert's eyes roved around him, rested for a moment on the beaver house, and then flicked frantically up the pond. No, he had no better place to hide. "Please, please, let 'em go away!" he silently pleaded.

"And here it is," came a voice just over his head, followed by a startled "Hey!" Instinctively, Bert made a dive for the water, and began to swim out into the pond with smooth, strong strokes. As he splashed through the water, he could hear enraged shouts behind him. Then there was the screaming splash of a bullet hitting the water; and, at the same moment, he dived after filling his lungs with air. How he did it, he could never afterward tell, but just at the moment he thought his lungs would burst, he brushed a flailing hand against something compounded of mud and sticks—the beaver house! With the air that remained in his lungs, he summoned enough energy to feel his way around. His hand encountered space. It was the entrance to the beaver house. He rammed his head through the entranceway and poked it up into life-giving air. Wet and shivering, he managed to hold himself steady against the muddy platform, and opened his eyes. Light filtered dimly through the beaver house; the air was stale and damp, but it could be breathed. His teeth were chattering from the chill of the water; his clothes were drenched; and now, with the excitement over, his injured heel was beginning to pain him again.

How long he clung there in the beaver house, Bert did not know. His watch had absorbed water and stopped. Outside, there was only a great silence, but it was followed by the sharp crack of a shot. The sound stirred Bert to action.

"I can't stay here forever," he reminded himself.

He filled his lungs with air once more and plunged out into the water. He was careful to feel his way to the surface, and to keep the beaver house between him and the shore. Cautiously, he pulled himself up on the side of the house, and peered toward the campsite. What he saw quickened his heart. Ed and Howard were pouring pails of water on the smouldering tent; the hermit was moving around the campsite, looking at the ground. And the Wallaces were nowhere in sight!

He let himself down in the water again, and began to swim toward shore. He knew what his brothers were thinking. They thought the Wallaces had taken him away, but, without a gun, Ed and Howard were helpless to do anything about it. His chest grated on the muddy shore, and he pulled himself out of the water. Very carefully, he climbed over the edge of the bank and walked toward Howard and Bert, whose backs were turned to him.

"Hello, fellows," he said, with elaborate casualness. He burst into a guffaw as they whirled around with expressions of amazement on their faces. Then they had encircled him, and their hands were beating his back. Howie was even crying a little.

"You're safe!" his younger brother blubbered. "You're safe, Bert!"

Bert had to agree that it was the best welcome home he had ever received.

CHAPTER TWENTY

"THEY'LL SURRENDER!"

The Wallaces had done a thorough job. Bert had to agree to that. What flour remained had been dumped on the ground. It took half an hour's searching to uncover the carefully camouflaged spots where the meat, the remainder of the sugar, and the canned goods had been buried. The Wallaces, in the belief that Bert had drowned, had strewn pine needles over each cache. It was necessary to keep a sharp eye out for places where the earth or the carpeting of brownish needles appeared to have been disturbed. And the tent? Well, a huge hole had been burned in one side of it, so that to sleep there would have been almost the same as sleeping outdoors, and equally bad on a rainy night. For some unexplained reason, the canoe had escaped. Perhaps, Bert suggested to his brothers, the joy of destruction around the campsite had occupied the Wallaces so thoroughly that they neglected the canoe until too late.

"Just what *did* happen?" he finally asked Ed. His brother, relaxed by now, sat down beside the evening campfire for a moment.

"Well, when you heard that shot," Ed told him,

"that was our little party coming back. We'd walked a long way in to the pond, and it was quite a distance to the other shore. Sure enough, we found the Wallace camp, but there wasn't anyone around. We sat there for quite a long time, hidden in the woods, waiting for them to come back. Finally it occurred to us that we might have missed them; that they might be down around our own camp. We ran most of the way back, Howie and I. Mr. Belton just walked, but he can walk as fast as we can run in these woods. When we got to the edge of the clearing, we saw the Wallaces. Mr. Belton fired one shot, as a warning, and they started to run. Mr. Belton followed them; but, apparently, they'd berthed a canoe downstream, and they got away from him."

"It surely was lucky that you came back when you did," Bert said soberly. He reached out a hand and laid it on his brother's arm. "Believe me, I thought I was finished."

"And I'll bet a buck that the Wallaces think you *were* finished," broke in Howard, who had strolled over after a rueful inspection of the tent. "They'd never think of the beaver house."

"Yeah, I was mighty lucky," Bert concurred. "And now I'm mighty drowsy. What're we going to do about that hole in the tent?"

"That's simple," called out the hermit, who was busy chopping down two sizable saplings on the edge of the clearing. Bert got to his feet, hobbling along because his heel still was sore, and walked over to Belton's side.

"See here," the hermit said to him. "We'll just lean these two poles against the side of the tent, tie some smaller poles crosswise, and then thatch the whole thing with balsam boughs. You'll sleep just as snug as if you had a whole tent again."

And, sure enough, when the three boys had completed the work of thatching, their tent was weathertight again. Just in time too, Bert realized. Drifting clouds had obscured the sparkling stars; in the distance, there was a faint rumble of thunder, and then a big drop of rain fell with a splash on his cheek.

"Gravy!" Bert said, jumping. "We'd better get inside before we get soaked." He propelled himself through the doorway of the tent, followed by his two brothers, and waited for the hermit to poke his shaggy, white head through. Instead, nothing happened. Bert poked his own head out the door and saw Belton move toward the edge of the clearing.

"Aren't you going to stay with us tonight?" he called out. His words almost were drowned by a peal of thunder, and then the blinding flash of a bolt of lightning.

"Later," called back the hermit. "Later. I've got some things to do."

"You're not going to try to find the Wallaces in

this storm, are you?" Bert asked loudly.

"I ain't sayin'," the hermit's voice came back to him. "Just let's say that I'm goin' on a little trip, and I'll be back before many hours have passed."

Bert pulled his head back inside the tent. The rain was beginning to pelt down, drumming on the canvas and dripping along the groundcloth outside.

"I'd certainly like to know what the hermit's got in mind," he said as he slid into his sleeping bag and let its warmth envelop him. There was no sound from his brothers. Both of them were asleep. Bert lay there, puzzling over the events of the day, and then he, too, dropped off to sleep.

Sometime late in the night, he woke again, sensing that something was going on. He could see the bulky form of the hermit as Belton spread out his blankets, lay down, and rolled up in them. He wanted desperately to find out what had happened; but, wisely, he held his tongue. Even before the hermit had begun to snore, Bert dropped off to sleep again.

Morning came in damply, with a fine mist sifting down through the trees and a shower of droplets tumbling from the branches as an occasional gust of wind swept through the clearing. The pond was hidden by fog; the fire crackled sullenly, giving off much smoke; but Belton was busy making breakfast when Bert finally opened his eyes and looked outside. Shivering a little in the penetrating cold, he drew on his socks, noting that his heel was better. He slipped into his clothes, pulled on his shoes, and then put a poncho over his head before venturing out-of-doors.

"Morning," the hermit greeted him, and held out a tin plate heaped with scrambled eggs and garnished with bacon. Bert accepted it gratefully, and took shelter under an unusually bushy tree, spooning up the warm food and then going back for more when the hermit assured him there was plenty. He still wanted to know what had happened the night before; but, by now, he had learned to let Belton tell him in his own good time.

"I kin see the look in your eyes," the hermit said, chuckling, as he sat down beside Bert. "But, no matter how much you want to know, I ain't goin' to tell you much about what happened last night."

"Well, can you tell me if you visited the Wallaces' camp?" Bert asked impatiently.

"Yes, that I did, son," the hermit admitted, gulping down a draft of steaming cocoa. "That I did. And I fixed 'em. In a couple more days, they'll be beggin' to surrender, to be arrested, and to be out of these woods."

"Well, how'd you do it?" demanded Bert, his curiosity thoroughly aroused. The only answer was another chuckle. "Wait and see," said the hermit.

"I Kin See the Look in Your Eyes."

"You'll see." And he got up and returned to the fire where Howard and Ed were standing, shivering, waiting for their breakfast. Bert shook his head, and proceeded to consume his breakfast.

"Well, now what?" Ed called across to him. Bert pretended to be sunk in thought.

"Let's get down to Eagle Lake," suggested the hermit. "We can talk to Will Thompson, the ranger down there. He'll come along with us when we pick up the Wallaces."

Bert laughed as he saw the amazed expression on his brothers' faces. He put a warning finger to his mouth as they turned to stare at him, and both of them wisely decided not to ask any questions.

In the mist, a little later, they loaded their canoe and set off down the pond. The hermit, once more, decided to walk. Islands and headlands loomed up like ghosts in the mist as Bert plied his paddle; the pond gave way to a winding stream. Strange birds took flight in the fog, frightened by the canoe, and then a weak sun began to pierce the opaque blanket that shut off the shores from view. Gradually the mist burned away, and blue sky once more came into sight.

"Ponchos off!" called Bert, pulling his own over his head, and letting the sun beat on his bare head and his tanned arms. For what he had been through the day before, it occurred to him, he felt pretty well. In fact, the whole trip so far had been a success, even considering what the Wallaces had tried to do to him.

The canoe swept around a bend in the river and revealed the prettiest campsite Bert had yet seen. On a high promontory a tent was pitched, with a fire crackling out in front. Alongside the promontory, a green stream foamed down through boulders, and then dropped over a ledge to splash into the main river. Two men were standing beside the fire, and Bert felt a twinge of recognition. Where had he seen that plaid shirt before? Suddenly, he knew.

"Jed!" he called. The taller of the two men whirled, and his face was split by a grin at the same moment he threw up his hand in recognition. The other man kept his back turned. They had caught up again, Bert realized, with Jed and young Grady. His suspicion of Grady was overbalanced by his happiness in seeing Jed again. He wanted to talk to the old guide, to tell him what had happened, and to ask his advice. He nodded to Ed, still paddling in the back of the canoe, and they swung in toward shore. Bert lit lightly on the sand, pulling the prow out of the water and up on the beach before he started up the bank with his hand outstretched. Jed met him at the top of the little rise. Just as Bert shook hands with him, he noted that Grady had crawled back into the tent. *Sullen fellow,* he thought to himself.

And I still don't trust him.

"What held you up?" Jed asked, and Bert caught himself just as he was about to pour out the whole story of their adventures. Instead, he took Jed by the arm and led him to the edge of the water. There, in a low voice, he explained how the Wallaces had tried to wreck their camp and to dispose of him. Jed's normally ruddy face grew even redder as he listened to the story, but he smiled in agreement as Bert mentioned the hermit's name.

"Nice fella, that," he finally said. "As long as he's keepin' track of you, nothin' bad will happen to you." He scratched his head, perplexed, when Bert told him the hermit's claim that he had fixed the Wallaces.

"I can't figger how," he mused, "but old fellers like Belton know a lot more about the woods, and people in the woods, than even we guides do. String along with him. Maybe he's wrong, but maybe he did do somethin' to tone 'em down."

"How about this fellow, Grady?" Bert asked, in a muted voice. "Have you been watching him?"

"Yeah," said Jed, his face clouding over. "I've been watchin' him, but one afternoon he got away from me. I dunno where he went, but he didn't come back until after dark, and he wouldn't tell me where he'd been."

"I can guess," Bert said bitterly. "But I can't

prove it. Just keep an eye on him a while longer."

"Sure will," Jed said, "and we'll see you again, downstream. There's a loggin' highway that comes in below Eagle Lake, on the next pond. Mebbe we can meet down there for one last talk. Mebbe," he hesitated, "mebbe by then the Wallaces will be out of your hair."

"I certainly hope so," said Bert earnestly, and shoved his canoe out into deeper water. He seated himself, lifted his paddle in a gesture of farewell, and dipped it into the green water. They were off again, and Eagle Lake was not very far away.

Ahead, Bert could see the river opening and the shores drawing back. A tiny island divided the stream, and the water rushed swiftly but smoothly by on both sides. As the canoe slid past, Bert could look farther into the distance.

"Eagle Lake!" he called back to his brothers, and pointed with his paddle. This was no mere widening of the river, but rather a real body of water. The far shore was perhaps six miles away, and on both sides little bays and inlets made a jigsaw pattern that, from the air, would have looked something like an eagle with outstretched wings. A steady breeze was blowing toward them, up the lake. The lee shore, out of the wind, was to their left. Great ledges sloped down to the water. On top of one of these out-croppings was a huge pile of logs.

"Must be a part of the lumbering operation," Bert suggested as he stopped paddling for a moment in the shelter of a tiny spit of land.

"Yeah, but why do they leave the logs up there?" asked Howard, displaying a practical interest in the processes of lumbering.

"Well, when they get enough of them stacked up," Bert concluded, "they'll roll them down into the water and then sluice them down through the dam at the foot of the lake to the sawmills downstream."

"Let's go closer and take a look at it," Howard suggested.

Bert was perfectly willing. The canoe glided along until it was directly underneath the pile of massive logs and a little distance out from shore.

"Sort of frightening, isn't it, fellows?" Bert called out. "I'd hate to think what those logs would do to you if they started rolling when you were underneath."

"Aw, you're just jittery since yesterday," Howard retorted. Bert stared up at the massive logs, a dubious look still in his eye.

"Just the same," he said, "it makes me nervous, and—"

"Look out!" came a yell from Ed, and the canoe shot forward as if all of them were racing for their lives. Bert cast one startled glance upward. The biggest of the logs, perched atop the pile, was moving. He dipped his paddle in with a mighty lunge. There was a rumbling crash and then a continuous staccato roar. The canoe was almost swamped by the mighty waves. Even in his panic, Bert managed to look back again. The whole pile of logs was tumbling into the water. Great spouts of spray shot into the air, and immense waves bore down on the canoe. For a moment Bert thought they were going to be swamped, and then they were riding clear on waves of lessening height.

"Let's get out of here!" he said grimly. "The Wallaces must be around!"

He applied himself to the paddle, and the canoe shot down the lake. Bert's back and arms began to ache, but still he kept on paddling furiously until, in the distance, he saw a log cabin on the lake shore, a wisp of smoke coming from its chimney.

"That's the ranger's cabin," he called back to his brothers. "We're safe now." He exhaled his breath with a mighty sigh, put his paddle across the canoe, and dropped his head on it. He was still shaken by his narrow escape.

As he resumed paddling, he saw a tall, thin man walking down the dock toward him. The canoe slid up alongside the pilings, and the man reached down to hold it steady as Bert climbed out.

"Howdy," he said with a smile. "I'm Will Thompson, the ranger here. And, whoever you fellows are, you're lucky. I heard those logs let loose, and I'm just about to go up to find out how it happened."

"Don't bother," Bert said as his brothers clambered from the canoe. "Somebody was trying to make trouble for us."

On the cool screen porch of the cabin, Bert told the whole story of the trip. Just as he finished, there was a tapping at the outer door.

"Mr. Belton!" Bert said, looking out through the mesh into the face of the hermit.

"I heard what happened to you," the hermit said as he came in and shook hands with Bert. "But don't worry. Those Wallaces will be surrenderin' within a day or two, mark my words!" He said it with such earnestness that Bert could not possibly doubt him.

CHAPTER TWENTY-ONE

THE STORM

"By the way," Will Thompson said, "I've got some food for you. Pete Harvey stopped by yesterday and told me you were running out of supplies."

"Gee, that's perfect," Bert exclaimed, following Thompson through the little cabin to the kitchen. In the excitement of the day's trip, he had forgotten all about Harvey's promise.

"How much longer you going to be out?" Thompson inquired, stroking his tanned face with his hand. He leaned up against the kitchen table, and looked quizzically at Bert.

"Well, if we don't have any more trouble, we should be able to finish in two weeks," Bert said, mentally reviewing the map distance from the ranger's cabin to the point where the river came out again into civilization. Thompson raised his eyebrows.

"Were you figuring on going all the way through to St. Thomas?" he asked, and Bert could sense that there was an unspoken question in his mind.

"Why—I guess so," Bert said, wondering why Thompson had asked him.

"I'm not sure that you'll be able to do it," Thompson explained. "You saw that they were lumbering up here on Eagle Lake, of course." Bert nodded. "Well," Thompson continued, "they may start driving logs down through there any day now. They've got logs backed up all the tributaries, too, and once the drive starts, you'll be stuck. In fact, I'm not sure you can get through ahead of the drive. Those logs really move, once they open up the dams."

"Gee whiz," Bert said, disappointed, "then what can we do? Will we have to turn around, or what?"

"No," said Thompson, bending down to pick up a heavy cotton sack full of groceries, which he handed to Bert. "The lumber company has a truck road down at the foot of Crow Lake, that's about two days' trip away, and they'll haul you back to the village, if you ask them."

"It seems a shame," said Bert, reflectively hefting the sack of supplies, "but I guess we've used up so much time, anyhow, that we might as well call it a day. That is—" he was struck by a thought, "if we catch the Wallaces first."

"I think I'd rely on the old hermit's promise," Thompson said as he started back toward the living-room. "He may seem a little queer, but he's taking an interest in you boys, and my guess is that he's got something good up his sleeve."

"Okay, then," agreed Bert. "I've been told that

The Ranger Handed Bert the Groceries

the lumber company has a dam down at the foot of Cross Lake, this side of Crow Lake. Isn't that right?" Thompson nodded assent.

"Then, I'll ask the caretaker there to phone ahead for a truck," Bert continued.

"That would be okay," said Thompson, who by this time was halfway through the door to the front porch, "but you seem to forget that today is Sunday. The boys will all be in town. You'd better just camp down on Cross Lake for the night, and go on to Crow Lake the next day. They'll be glad to help you down there, even without any advance notice."

Bert saw that his two brothers were sitting forward, listening to the conversation. He glanced quickly at Howard, then at Ed. "Seem okay to you?" he asked, dropping the sackful of supplies on a convenient table.

"Sure," they both chorused.

"But where's the hermit gone?" he asked, suddenly realizing that Belton was nowhere in sight.

"Oh, he borrowed an extra canoe and started down the lake," Ed volunteered. "Said he'd some investigating to do; he'll meet us tonight at the Cross Lake campsite."

"Well, then, let's go," Bert said briskly. He shook hands warmly with Thompson, who regarded him reassuringly. He picked up the bagful of supplies and walked down the pathway to the dock.

Behind him, Bert heard Thompson call out, "I'll be keeping an eye on you, too. Soon as Pete Harvey shows up, I'll send him on down to join you. Good luck—and good hunting."

Bert yanked one arm free from beneath the heavy load he was carrying, and waved acknowledgment. By now he was walking alongside the canoe. He carefully loaded the bagful of supplies, stepped nimbly in, and picked up his paddle.

The wind had shifted slightly, as it so often does, in the mountain country, and now was blowing directly up the lake. A faint haze had begun to collect around the sun, forerunner of another storm, and Bert had to paddle briskly. The breeze cooled his chest and bare arms, and he felt rested and reassured after the visit with the ranger.

Little islands dotted the lake; the boys slipped quickly by them and came out into an open stretch of water where the waves had begun to roll higher, cresting lazily, and cradling the canoe in their troughs.

"Thank goodness for the wind," Bert called back to Ed, who was occupied with his paddling. "It'll cut down the flies as long as we're out here on the water, anyway." Ed acknowledged the comment with a grin and kept on with his work. Bert felt a surge of affection for his older brother. Ed was a steady fellow; no doubt about that. And Howard, too—

impetuous Howie, usually—but, on this trip, Bert had been the impetuous one. He took a mental vow to be more prudent hereafter, and, at the same moment, knew that if a project caught his attention, he'd be dashing off headlong to try it again.

Gradually the shores of the lake were closing in, and the mutter of tumbling water could be heard directly ahead. Bert cast a mental look at the map, and recalled that these rapids were negotiable. He paddled straight ahead until the current caught the canoe, and then worked with precision and skill as the shiny metal craft shot down through the funnels of water, dodged dizzily around fanglike rocks, and finally slid out again into a bubbling eddy. They were back on the river now, and the breeze lessened. Lazily Bert dipped his paddle as they moved downstream.

At noon, with the hazy sun high overhead, he pointed toward the shore, and they moved crosscurrent to make camp. It was a lazy lunch; Bert slept a few minutes after it was over, and found himself strangely reluctant to get back in the canoe. He forced himself to do so, however, and lengthening afternoon shadows found the three boys dropping down through another noisy rapids to their campsite at the head of Cross Lake.

Here was a wider, longer body of water than any they had seen so far. Off in the distance, Bert caught the dull glint of logs bobbing on the ripples. The storm, apparently, had subsided. There was almost a flat calm. The sun was still obscured, and fish-shaped clouds were moving in from the north. Unless the weather changed quickly before morning, Bert concluded, they would be in for a hard paddle.

"Okay, let's unload!" he called out as the canoe grated on the bank. With a speed born of practice, he lifted out two duffle bags and tossed them up in the grassy clearing. As his brothers toted up the other bags and the carefully folded tent, he looked around for the hermit. Belton was nowhere in sight. He glanced down the lake. For a moment, he thought he saw the movement of a canoe. Perhaps that was Belton, still looking for the Wallaces.

"I'm going down the lake a little distance," he announced. His brothers turned startled faces toward him.

"Oh, I won't get out of sight," he said hastily, by way of amending his original remark. "I thought I saw Mr. Belton down there, and, if I did, I'd like to talk to him."

"Well, be careful," he heard Ed say, grudgingly.

Bert nodded. "I will," he answered as he jumped into the stern of the canoe and dipped his paddle in the water. He noted that the fishing tackle was still strapped to the thwarts on one side of the canoe. A light breeze, this time from behind him, sprang up as he slid away from the shore and made for an island where a lone pine stood like a sentinel. He was paddling slowly, watching what went on around him. Suddenly, just ahead, there was a heavy splash, and a lake trout rose out of the water to snap at a dancing fly.

"Oh, boy!" Bert said to himself. "Supper!" He quickly unstrapped the fishing tackle, put on an oversize Royal Coachman, and cast into the clear waters. Almost immediately he had a strike. The lake trout fought bitterly, boring down toward the bottom, dipping under the canoe in a vain effort to untangle the line, but gradually weakening. Finally, Bert brought him alongside the boat, deftly inserted a thumb in the fish's gill, and neatly flipped him into the canoe. He was a beauty, about an eight-pounder, Bert estimated.

Again and again he cast, but there seemed to be no more fish in the area. Ahead of him, about a mile distant, he could see a larger island. He paddled quickly toward it; and, on a shoal offshore, caught another trout. Glancing behind him, he could see the handkerchief-size campsite where, no doubt, his brothers by now had set up the tent and were chopping wood for the fire. Down the lake, there was no sign of another canoe; nothing, in fact, but the lazily bobbing logs.

There was a rumble of thunder overhead. Bert

looked up, startled. Black clouds were pouring across the sun; and, off on one corner of the horizon, a knifelike bolt of lightning flickered feebly. As Bert swung the canoe around, to start back to camp, the first squall hit. Poised as he was, in the back of the canoe, he was in the worst possible place to maneuver. His weight had lifted the bow, and the first waves hit it with such force that, despite his best efforts, the craft was wrenched sidewise in the waves. Then there was calm, for a moment, during which he managed to struggle forward on hands and knees to the center of the canoe, where he knelt, gasping, and began to wield his paddle again.

Crash! another bolt of lightning, and rain began to pour down. Behind it came the wind. The shores were blotted out by a driving sheet of water; the waves began to rise to mountainous size. The wind came in gusts. During each gust, Bert had to paddle feverishly to keep from going backward. Between gusts, he might make a few feet of progress. His arms were beginning to ache, and there was a dull throbbing in his back. By now the wind was howling. Off on shore, he could hear the splintering sound of a tree being wrenched from its anchorage by the force of the wind. His arms were growing more and more heavy.

"I—I can't stand it!" he finally gasped. The wind and waves were too much for him. With a swift thrust of his paddle, he swung the canoe around. He would have to run with the wind until the storm was over. Perhaps he could take refuge in some cove. Perhaps he might even be able to reach some sort of cabin down by the dam. He still had to paddle to keep the canoe from swinging into the trough of the waves, but now and then the rain stopped momentarily, and he could see the shores sliding by him. For a long period of time, now, he had been running alongside high, sandy bluffs without a single opening into which he could slide the canoe for shelter. He conceded, grudgingly, that he would have to go all the way to the end of the lake.

The rain beat down again, and the wind resumed its shrill, whistling noise. The waves were higher now; the canoe would poise precariously on a crest, begin to slide into the trough; and then Bert would have to paddle like mad to keep it on the right course before it rose again on the side of another massive wave. He had just topped one towering crest, and was dipping his paddle for the stroke that would keep him on the right course, when there was a grinding noise. The canoe stopped abruptly, lurched, and Bert found himself floundering in the water. He thrust out one hand, and it touched something slippery. He had crashed into the logs head-on, and now it was no longer a question of keeping the canoe afloat. It was a question of his own life!

Over his head, a massive log poised threateningly; he took two frantic strokes and moved out of the way just in time. Gasping for breath, he put out his hand again. This time, it caught on a stub projecting from another log. Painfully, hardly knowing what he was doing, he pulled himself free of the water. And, just then, the wind died again. Astraddle the log, he pushed the dripping hair from his eyes and looked around him. He was on the edge of the run of logs; if he could manage to paddle free, he would be blown in to shore.

Dipping his hands into the water as the calm continued, he managed to pull his log away from the heaving mass that lay to his right. Then the wind struck again, and he needed to do no more. The towering waves sped him toward shore; there was a lurch as his log struck bottom, and he was thrown free. A great comber hurled him up toward the sand. As it receded, he dragged himself, clawing and kicking, farther up the beach and out of range of the battering waves. As he lay there, trying to get back the energy he had expended, he could hear the dull, thudding noise of the waves beating on the beach; and, now and then, a splintering crack as a log was split in two.

How long he rested, he did not know. Finally, his wet clothing clinging to his body, he got to his feet and looked around him. The rain was still beating down; but, between the driving sheets of water, he spied a light. Luck had brought him to a cabin! Very slowly he climbed a bank, stumbled up the steps, and beat on the massive front door. Just that little gesture, raising his hand to knock, drained out the last of the ebbing store of energy that had carried him through the storm. Very slowly he slid down against the door. The last he remembered was that the door opened, that somebody picked him up in strong arms, and that he was lying on a bed.

When Bert awoke, hours later, the storm was still beating against the walls of the cabin; outside the trees were shuddering and groaning; rain poured down the windows. Raising himself on an elbow, he looked about him. He was alone, but he could hear movement in the kitchen. Very slowly he sat up and looked at his watch. It was eight at night!

A swinging door separated the kitchen from the living-room. On the walls a logger's sharp-pointed peavey, used to separate logs, showed him that he must have reached the gatekeeper's cabin. He could faintly hear the rumble of voices on the other side of the door. As he sat upright in the bunk, the door opened.

The grin on Bert's face froze into a grimace of fear. His heart began to thud. He looked frantically around him. The man in the door was none other

The Man in the Door Was Tom Wallace!

than Tom Wallace!

"Welcome," said Wallace, an evil smile on his face. "Welcome to our little cabin, young man. Enjoying yourself here?"

Bert tried to answer, but the only sound that came from his choked throat was a feeble croak. He pulled himself back against the wall and sat staring fascinated at his enemy. As Wallace pulled up a chair and sat down by a fireplace across the room, the kitchen door opened. It was Alan.

"Nice to see you again," he said in a deep, grumbling voice. "Although you may not think so before we get done with you."

"What are you going to do?" Bert croaked. He was trapped, and he was frightened.

"Wait and see," said Alan, rubbing his hands. "Wait until the storm's over, and you'll see."

Bert dropped back and stretched out full-length in the bunk, his back toward the two Wallaces. *What can I do?* he asked himself. He knew the answer before he asked the question. There was nothing he could do.

CHAPTER TWENTY-TWO

THE GATEKEEPER'S CABIN

If Bert slept at all during the remainder of the night, he did not remember. It seemed to him that he was awake continuously; and, each time he looked toward the fireplace, either Alan or Tom Wallace was staring evilly back at him. Outside the storm still rattled the windows. As a gray and watery dawn began to lighten the sky, Bert realized that the gusts were diminishing in their intensity.

Sometime before six o'clock, Tom Wallace got up heavily and went to the kitchen. Bert could hear the rattling of dishes as the old prospector fed himself; he returned with a plateful of food for Alan, who by this time was awake in his bunk. Bert must have looked hopeful, for Wallace leered at him and said hoarsely, "You won't need to eat this morning." The old man chuckled, and the sound struck a chill to Bert's heart.

Finally, as the day began to brighten outside, Tom Wallace turned to his son, and Bert heard him say, "We'd better get goin'. The keeper will be back soon, about eight o'clock, I'd judge. We'll have to be away by then." Alan glanced at Bert through narrowed eyelids, and then whispered something to his grizzled father.

"Oh, yes," said Wallace. "Son, we want all the fly dope you're carryin' with you."

"But I haven't any!" Bert protested, swinging his feet out of the bunk. Somehow, just to stand upright gave him more courage.

"Don't give us that!" snarled the elder Wallace, striding across the room. "Turn out your pockets!" Bert turned every pocket inside out. The old man patted his trouser legs and then burst into a shout of rage.

"Don't let it worry you, Dad," Alan said, but Bert seemed to detect a note of shakiness in the younger man's voice. "We'll get along all right."

"Yeah, we'll have to," Tom Wallace said bitterly. "But ain't that just our luck?"

He wheeled on Bert and almost spat out his words. "Stand still, boy," he said. "We got something to do." From his pockets, he produced a length of cord and tied Bert's hands behind him.

"March," he ordered brusquely, flinging open the front door.

It would be folly to resist, Bert realized. He walked slowly toward the dock that extended out into the lake. The gale had been replaced by a damp, clinging mist. He could see the black flies, gathering in clouds around his head. They would hover there a moment, scent the fly dope that was still plastered thickly on his face, and then buzz away. Now and then he could hear Tom Wallace, behind him, slap at his neck and grumble. He wondered, idly, why Wallace didn't smear on some of his own fly dope. *If he had any—if—* Bert began to wonder.

"Get in that canoe," said Wallace, and Bert obediently stepped down into a canoe that bobbed alongside the dock. Alan climbed in behind him, and soon they were gliding out toward the farther edge of the logs. For one wild moment Bert thought of upsetting the canoe, but he abandoned that. His arms were tied, he was fully dressed, and he would sink to the bottom. He could not swim out of this predicament, that was certain.

"So long," said Alan, climbing out of the canoe and balancing himself nimbly on a large log.

"What're you going to do?" Bert demanded huskily. Even helpless as he was, he felt a surge of rage. He moved his arms; they were tightly bound.

"Wait and see," called Alan, jumping from log to log until finally he was ashore again. Bert looked up at the dam. Through a momentary gap in the mist, he could see Tom Wallace at work there. He was turning something, he was—he was opening the gates! Despair swept over Bert. The canoe began to move, very slowly, drifting along with the logs. In a few minutes, Bert knew, he would be part of a grinding, tossing mass of logs, swept down through the dam. *Helpless,* he said bitterly to himself.

Again the mist swept aside. Overhead there was a roaring sound, a familiar sound. At first, Bert did not quite recognize it. Then he knew. Pete Harvey was coming in to land! The canoe was still moving slowly toward the dam. Above the noise of the plane's motor, he heard Alan shout to his father in a voice pitched high by fear.

"Let's get out of here! We've got no guns. Let's run!" And, as the mist swirled and eddied, Bert saw Tom Wallace's stooped figure as the old prospector fled from the crest of the dam. The roar of the plane subsided, but the logs were moving faster, and Bert was caught up in their slow, steady progress. Ahead of him, he could see the open gate of the dam before the mist closed in again. The noise of the falling water was growing louder. And then, as he numbly gave himself up to his fate, he was no longer moving. Someone was running out on the logs. It was Ed!

"Ed!" he yelled. His brother was balancing delicately on a huge pine spar and leaning over to fumble with the knots at his wrists. "Ed!" He began to cry. His wrists were free now, and he could feel the blood flow back into them.

"Come on, kid," Ed said gruffly to him. "You're all right now." Balancing himself, with Ed's help, he made his way to the shore. Howard was waiting there. So were Belton and Pete Harvey, all of them grinning with relief.

"We got you just in time," Harvey said as he stuck out his hand and pumped Bert's arm.

"What'd you do, close the gate again?" Bert asked breathlessly.

"Yeah," said Harvey. "That's why the logs stopped moving. It was just in time, too."

"But how'd you know where I was?" Bert asked, as he moved toward the gatekeeper's cabin.

"Oh, Mr. Belton here was scouting down the lake yesterday afternoon, and he saw the Wallaces moving down toward the cabin. Guess they realized that the keeper would be away on Sunday. He came back to tell us, and we would have started last night, but the storm was too bad. I know this country pretty well, so I navigated my way down here in the mist today." The pilot flung open the door to the cabin, and Bert stumbled inside.

"I'm hungry," he said. Ed and Howard sprinted for the kitchen. "Fire's still burning," they called back. "Breakfast in a few minutes."

Bert relaxed in a chair and closed his eyes. He was really tired now. It seemed only seconds later when someone shook his shoulder, and he looked up into Ed's eyes. His older brother was holding out a steaming cup of hot milk and a plate full of scrambled eggs. Bert drank down the scalding milk, and forked up the scrambled eggs almost mechanically. Then he closed his eyes and went back to sleep.

The slamming of a door awoke him, and he looked up drowsily at the towering figure of Jed. Behind the guide, he could see Bob Grady. Both of them were grinning. Grady came forward and stuck out his hand. Bert accepted it automatically, but coldly.

"I guess I owe you an apology," Grady said, kneeling down beside the chair. "You thought I was mixed up with the Wallaces, didn't you?"

"Well, yes," Bert confessed. "You certainly acted as if you were."

"Now I can tell you," Grady said. "Now that the Wallaces won't be bothering any of us any more." Very swiftly, Grady sketched the story of his days at school. A watch was missing. As a matter of routine, the headmaster had made a search of every boy's possessions. In Grady's dresser, the watch had been found. He was innocent, but he had been expelled from school.

"I always suspected Alan Wallace of playing that dirty trick on me," he said, "but I kept my suspicions to myself. When I saw him in Boston, not long ago, I managed to find out where he was going. I thought I'd trail along, so I got Jed as a guide and started downriver, following them. Then, when you

"I Guess I Owe You an Apology, Bert."

fellows showed up, things got so complicated that I didn't know exactly what to do."

"Well, I guess it doesn't matter now," Bert said heartily. A sudden thought occurred to him, and he looked across the room at the old hermit, who was stroking his white whiskers. "But what about the Wallaces now?" he called. Belton winked at him.

"Just wait," he said. "Just go back to sleep, and wait."

Bert drowsily closed his eyes and tipped his head back against the cushion on the back of the chair. When he woke again, the cabin was deserted. Everybody had gone. He got up painfully, flung open the front door, walked out on the porch and down the path, and sat meditatively on the dock. Lumbermen were at work across the pond. He could hear the shrill whine of their saws, and occasionally the crash of a falling tree, but he could not see them.

Then, across the dam in the failing afternoon sunlight, a strange procession began to march. At its head were Tom and Alan Wallace. By looking sharply, he could see that their hands were tied. Marching just behind the Wallaces, his head thrown back proudly, was the old hermit. Behind him, in turn, were Howard, Ed, and Pete Harvey.

"We got 'em!" Howard called out cheerily.

Bert ran toward the dam and met the little procession. The two Wallaces scowled at him. Their faces were marked by dozens of reddish swellings. *Fly bites,* Bert said to himself.

"Where'd you get 'em?" Bert asked eagerly as he walked alongside Harvey. The pilot smiled down at him.

"They were trying to steal a truck and get away, but some of the lumberjacks stopped 'em," he said. "They couldn't stand it any longer in the woods."

Bert let out a whoop, and threw his arms around the white-bearded hermit.

"Now I understand!" he shouted. "You took their fly dope and you hid their rifle that night you were scouting around their camp."

"That's right," said the hermit quietly. "I knew they couldn't live long in these woods with the flies bitin' the way they were. And the only way they could get out was to take to the loggin' road. So we just spread and waited."

"And now?" asked Bert. "What happens now?"

"Well, I'll put them in my plane and fly them back to the village," Pete Harvey said. "They've got plenty to answer for, interfering with the dams along the river, trying to harm you boys. We'll let a judge and jury decide how to punish 'em. Now, march!" He swung the Wallaces out of line, and down to the dock, where another canoe was moored.

"Well, and what do we do?" Bert asked as the rest of the party walked up the steps to the cabin, and settled down in the living-room.

"Go home!" chorused his brothers. Bert threw up his hands in a gesture of mock defeat.

"I guess you're right," he acknowledged. "Our own canoe is gone, they may start driving logs any day, and I guess we've had enough adventure to last us for a while."

There was a roaring sound outside. Bert ran to the door. Pete Harvey was warming up his plane. The pilot stuck one arm out a window and waved in farewell, then began to taxi down the water.

"There goes one of our best friends, and two of our enemies," said Bert, waving back. "But we boys have nothing to worry about now."

"Yeah," broke in Howard, his eyes twinkling as he came forward to stand beside his brother. "Now, let's go home and see what it's like to spend a quiet summer."

The loud honking of a horn broke in on the conversation.

"There's our truck," Ed said. "Let's go!" He flung his arm around Bert's shoulder, and they went out through the door, across the dam, and up to the waiting truck.

WHITMAN BOOKS
FOR BOYS AND GIRLS

NEW STORIES
OF ADVENTURE AND MYSTERY

Up-to-the-minute novels for boys and girls about favorite characters, all popular and well known—

ROY ROGERS and the Outlaws of Sundown Valley
ROY ROGERS and the Ghost of Mystery Rancho
ROY ROGERS and the Gopher Creek Gunman
ROY ROGERS and the Raiders of Sawtooth Ridge

GENE AUTRY and the Golden Ladder Gang
GENE AUTRY and the Thief River Outlaws
GENE AUTRY and the Redwood Pirates

ZANE GREY'S The Spirit of the Border
ZANE GREY'S The Last Trail

RED RYDER and the Adventure at Chimney Rock
RED RYDER and the Secret of the Lucky Mine

BLONDIE and DAGWOOD'S Adventure in Magic
BLONDIE and DAGWOOD'S Marvelous Invention

WHITMAN BOOKS
FOR BOYS AND GIRLS

NEW STORIES
OF ADVENTURE AND MYSTERY

The books listed above may be purchased at
the same store where you secured this book.